Mandragora

Autumnalis

Publisher: Lina Anthia E. Deligia

Author: Lina Anthia E. Deligia

E-mail: seizethedream2010@gmail.com

Greek Title Original: Μανδραγόρας Ο Φθινοπωρινός

English title: Mandragora Autumnalis

Copyright © Lina Anthia E. Deligia

Copyright © for the photos Front & Back Cover Lina Anthia E. Deligia

Cover Editor: Lina Anthia E. Deligia

Athens, October 2020

ISBN978-618-00-2565-1

Lina E. Deligia

Mandragora

Autumnalis

Lina was born and raised in Veria, a small town of Greece, in May of 1986. She has been working in tourism since she was eighteen and holds a degree in University of Business Administration & Economics. She has traveled to many parts of the world, while now living permanently in Athens, with her husband and her beloved dog! The short novel 'Mandragoras' is her first published work.

To Socrates, who was bringing me chocolates and colored pencils...

& to Magas who is always by my side...

Sections

Dreamy Journeys

New York, 24.07.2020

She met him when the hotel opened, after the pandemic. "Maybe instead of Canada I should go to Russia, Putin wants me at his side." The old man said. He knew quantum mechanics, the theory of relativity, astrophysics and writing, as he had already published six books before he even reached the age of thirty. He was a mathematician himself, with a war hero father. He had divorced his first wife because she was a Satanist and had gained many pounds in their last years as a couple. He knew Feynman and at the age of seven, he read 'Les Miserables' of Victor Hugo. Overall he knew nine languages and just as she had made sure, he was crazy and a storyteller; he started talking to her in perfect English and then in French and then the two of them talked in German. The conversation in German lasted several minutes and she confessed to him that she had always wanted to study at the University of Munich. That she could go and that it was her choice not to do so. This, of course, was a lie, because she simply did not have the money to study abroad! Mr. Avery was 72 years old, of medium height and always held his cane since he was almost blind in one eyes. She heard him coming from afar and prepared the key to his room. Mr. Avery, according to Jamie, was the most interesting customer to ever pass by that hotel. In a way, though, through their conversations, Jamie felt a little disadvantaged. It felt bad that he knew from astrophysics while she did not, badly for the pounds that his wife had gained, because she herself had gained some lately, bad that while she knew how to answer him intelligently in their discussions, she did not really know physics or mathematics, like he did. He made her feel bad about her choice not to study abroad. But most of all, Mr. Avery made her feel jealous. Every time they finished talking and he had left to his room, Jamie would sit at the front desk, thinking she should be reading more books.

She was even annoyed by the fact that he corrected her in German, because Jamie knew the language fluently, you see. Maybe not so perfectly after all, since Mr. Avery was right when he corrected her. How is it possible for a person to know so much, to have accumulated such a volume of information in his head, to be 72 years old and to remember everything, while she had forgotten yesterday's dinner? She thought. Mr. William Avery was one of the clients that the employees do not pay much attention to, as he seems, the truth is, a little crazy, but for our Jay he was important. She gave him all the attention he required and wanted to impress him with her knowledge. Whatever the knowledge was! Jamie still felt like a child. She was of course thirty-four years old, she had studied, she knew three languages and she was now learning the fourth, she had traveled to many places that others only dreamed of and she had already been working in tourism for the last thirteen years, but she remained a child at heart. The skills she acquired all these years working in the best hotels of New York and Europe, her deep knowledge and the many years of experience in the field, were certainly much more than what one needed to work, in the three star hotels where she worked at the moment. She knew that. Everything in it reminded her, after all. The rooms, the Lobby, her colleagues, even the customers who wondered themselves every now and then ... Maybe she was staying there, because she was tired of packing, she was thinking. Maybe she stayed, because the environment she encountered was nothing like the previous ones in which she used to work. This one was difficult from the very beginning and so she put a bet with herself. She would not allow anyone to say that she is spoiled or that she gives up easily. She was angry about that too. On the other hand, she was grateful and she especially appreciated Mrs. Orwell, for whom she worked. All this reminded her of those beautiful times in the luxury hotels of Greece, when she was highly regarded, when she was praised for her skills and development and she was being offered promotions, houses with private pools, plenty of money and the most promising of all, a very bright future! She remembered walking down a street with a long row of tall exotic palm trees. The leaves cast shadows on her every step and the light summer breeze made sure she reaches her shift cool! The view in those resort hotels, she usually worked in, was breathtaking! Even from her post at the reception, the view was unique, as all you could see in front of you was the deep blue of the sea joining the light blue of the sky. Those hotels also had luxurious Beach Bars, so beautiful with their palm trees, coconuts for decor and white furniture that invited you to lay on them and get lost on the endless canvas in front of you! Necessary company, the fruity cocktail offered to you by the sunburned bodies who worked at the beach bar, always accompanied by their smile! In the evenings, Jamie would take a walk on the island, enjoying her free time outside the hotel; she would taste the local cuisine and go out for that drink with her Latin colleague who seemed to be interested in her! These hotels usually employed people from all over the world, mainly from areas where the salary was much lower. Jamie did it for the experience but also for she needed a rich Vitae Curriculum that would open any door she wanted in the future. So every summer she would prepare her suitcase to visit exotic islands and foreign places. Jamie really liked this mix of cultures. She liked the fact that for six months she would only speak foreign languages, she liked traveling a lot and that gave her the idea she was on a vacation somewhere and had the opportunity to know a different culture! Every day she hung out inside and outside work, with Greeks, Romanians, Czechs, Nigerians, Brazilians and many other boys and girls! They would all gather together at night in the beach, lit fires and fell in love under the moon that was looking down on them and seemed to envy them a little.

Who wouldn't be jealous after all, even a little... when... 'track track track zzzzrfttk', the abrupt sound of the old fan on her feet, interrupted her thoughts. Now she was afraid of abandoning her completely and closed it for a while to let it rest. It is the third summer this fan is by her side working non-stop and the only way to cool down a bit during these hot days of July. She sat back down and tried to keep her eyes open this time, but in vain. The hot air coming from the open entrance of the hotel caused her intense dizziness and drowsiness and within a few minutes Jamie had already fallen asleep. The sound of a cane hitting the sidewalk was heard from afar and began to grow louder when, "I was told to come here, you are a good girl and you will help me. Is not that right?" he said in his thunderous voice, visibly agitated.

Jamie "Welcome! Where were you Mr. Avery, it has been some time now! "

Mr. Avery "You have to hide me because they will kill me, Petkov found out where I am and they will make it look like a car accident. Tonight we have business, call the leader to tell him that I have arrived safe."

Jamie realized it was a bad day for Mr. William. She was saddened by the fact that a man with so much knowledge and several diplomas had gone actually crazy! Ilona, Petkov's Bulgarian prostitute, knew who he was, she had seen him. So Jamie naturally, had to calm him down! Mr. Avery wanted to spend the night at the hotel, but last time he had left without paying, so Jamie told him he would have to prepay to stay, something Mr. Avery did not like at all! After all he was one of their best customers! They talked for a while, when he now had to be politely kicked out of the hotel. As he was leaving, she asked him if he had any children, hoping that there was someone in the world who cared about him. Then Mr. Avery snorted and said to her, "Isaac and little..." making his cross as a good Christian, "Ronda" and his blue old eyes filled with tears and closed as he walked away from the entrance. Jamie had already regretted it. She then remembered her own father, who is in Germany and she misses him, but also her mother who hasn't call her for many months now. Rarely their relationship was good. A constant drama out of nowhere, sometimes they overcame the quarrel relatively quickly and sometimes every effort seemed futile. Jamie was already going through a hard time in her life and this relationship she had now formed with her mother, cost her quite emotionally. She was like that from a young child; she expected to receive love, which other children her age have had so naturally and when she did not receive it the way she thought she should, Jamie felt sad and angry at the same time. This bothered her a lot and she was often melancholic whenever she thought about it. She was also greatly annoyed by the ingratitude of people and that is why not many good friends were left in her life. This, but also the fact that they all had to be compared to her best friend, her dog Axel! It was rare for someone to understand the special relationship Jamie and Axl had and surely our heroine does not expect anyone to understand her feelings towards this beautiful creature! She knows that what they have is unique and incomprehensive to most of the humans around her. Axl Rose, named after her favorite rock band, entered her life in May 2004, shortly before she left for studies. She has always loved animals much more than humans and that has not changed a bit to this day. Axl from that moment on would follow her everywhere! He would have all her attention and love! No one would dare to hurt him, for she protected him like a lioness mother! They would travel together, study together; she would take him along in the seasonal hotels where she worked, almost every summer and where they would swim on the sea; they would eat together every day and sleep together every night. Axel from the moment he was born became the center of her world and her whole universe! It was difficult for them to have such a perfect relationship to get all the love and true friendship they needed from each other and allow somebody else to enter into their companionship! And yet it happened! Sean would be the third person to join their company timidly and manage to love them even more, something neither of them thought was possible! Thus, with Axel and Jamie, Sean would learn what it means to love.

The sun had set but Jamie felt she had just got there for her shift as time seemed to fly away. Mr. Avery's company helped time pass faster and now she was looking forward to returning home. She hasn't got any sleep lately and really hoped to do so tonight. Axl's crises had subsided and everything indicated that today would be a quiet day. Some people have peace of mind and quite nights, whereas in the house of Jamie and Sean, the reality was very different!

The trial

New York, 28.02.2018

The creepy sound of Axel's small body hitting the wooden floor uncontrollably woke them up from a deep sleep. Foams came out of his mouth as his little head hit the floor again and again. His body was overwhelmed by an eerie force and his bladder had become an instrument of a mind without power. Without any thought they both ran next to him. It was the scariest moment of their lives. As the urine flooded the floor and Axl's mouth closed tightly, the very bad idea of putting her hand in the dog's mouth to prevent it from drowning, came to her mind and without any hesitation she threw it between the his jaws. The pain was unbearable, but the fear that something bad would happen to her little friend, surpassed in intensity any other emotion at that moment. His jaws were sealed and now the frighteningly pointy fangs were forcibly inserted into her skin, piercing it. Sean in a state of panic shouted at her "do not put it inside, baby no! He will smash it!" while Jamie started stroking him, kissing his velvety muzzle, begging him to calm down seconds before Axl finally released her hand.

The tears flowed endlessly on their faces and suddenly his jaws opened, his body regained the elasticity it had before and then Axl started barking and crying and Jamie's heart broke! Sean was terrified and was afraid to hold him alone while Jamie was getting quickly dressed to take him to the Vet. Watching Sean in shock, she shouted at him "You can do it! Are you listening?! You can do everything for Axel. Pull yourself together! " Sean knew this, however at that moment feeling so scared; he simply needed someone to remind it him. That day, they left panicking for the vet, wearing their pajamas and passed by, god knows, how many red traffic lights, while honking at pedestrians and others on their way to let them pass! Their baby needed them and they would do anything to protect it.

 Arriving at the vet clinic, they entered holding their little dog in their arms tightly, as if they had their own heart in their hands! They were afraid of the worst. Fate felt sorry for them and Axl lived. However, from that moment on it would test their endurance daily! Axl had a severe epileptic seizure and would later be taking heavy medication for the rest of his life. Almost every day, from there on, for their small family would be painful and scary. It would take them a long time to manage all this and when they would seem to succeed, the next crisis would knock on their door, reminding them that they will never get rid of it! The first year was very difficult and it would test their strength! Once a crisis left Axl, a very difficult week of adjustment followed as partial blindness and deafness and constant crying were among the main consequences of the epilepsy. Jamie endured everything, but she could not bear Axl's long and incessant crying. So as a superhero, Sean would take their little one to rest his beloved a little longer. Sean couldn't stand Axl's crying either, but you see, it hurt more to watch Jamie suffer, so it was a one-way street for him. Every month they turned their house into a fortress made of pillows, thus protecting every corner of the house so that their Axel would not hit during those seizures!

The second year, just as they had become familiar with the concept of epilepsy and had been informed about everything related to it, came full of suffering and intended to test their love! To all the above, more problems were added. Axle's pills had to be changed; he also had to take a higher dose which leads to more severe mental disorders, as the main drug to treat epilepsy is Phenobarbital, a substance that keeps the body in deep repression. Axel, now severely affected by drugs, had lost all restraint and began to fill the carpets of the house and every corner with his urine. Rare were the days when the couple would wake up and the house would not be covered with poo and urine. Jamie was the one who always came home first after work and had to deal with this situation more often. The truth is that she could not stand it anymore. Tired and hungry, exhausted just at the idea of what awaited her at home, she used to cry and clean their home for hours till the very next day. The Groundhog Day, as she so sadly used to say! The situation was no longer under control. Sean often woke up and saw her crying. She was crying because she was tired. She cried because she could no longer bear to wake up in this chaos. She could no longer stand another minute without any sleep. She could no longer bear Axl's crying. She felt useless. She could not help it. But most of all, she cried because she was afraid. She was afraid of losing her best buddy. That summer was the worst for Sean and Jamie, because they almost lost him. The crises were many, many and strong and the couple felt helpless! The vet threw up his hands and the phrase that came out of his mouth still haunts Jamie's dreams, "Jay, you need to be prepared for the worst. We can do nothing else." It must have been Jamie herself who managed to get him up on his feet again as she did not leave him alone even for a minute that day. She was looking down on him like a true guardian angel, like a mother protects her sick child. You see, you have to understand something. Axl and Jamie loved each other. From the first moment they met they were inseparable! Axl was the only constant in Jamie's life and her daily choice to love and protect him as much as he loved and protected her. Her parents were divorced, her father leaved in Germany and her mother with her husband in Poughkeepsie. Jamie's grandparents, from her father's side, were also staying in Poughkeepsie. When she got accepted in Emerson College, she had to move to Boston for her studies. So she left her childhood love behind in her hometown with a heavy heart, but Axl followed her! There was no doubt for that. Jamie's friends were constantly changing; the only friend however that never changed was Axl! Boyfriends were also many, the only constant love in her life though was her little Axel. You see in every change in her life, in every disappointment, in every move, the only constant in the life of both of them, was the love they had for each other! And the greatest feeling she had ever felt in her life, was now in danger of being lost! For that she cried and as much as she was trying to get her mind away of bad thoughts, her mind disobeyed and did its own thinking ...

The third year had already made its appearance and things had somewhat been normalized as the situation at home had calmed down. Christmas was in the spotlight, Jamie's favorite holiday and the atmosphere was festive and joyful. They hoped for better days but did not know as the year was changing and they were clinking their glasses together, that this third year would test their soul itself. January was coming in and Axl lost the mobility of his hind legs. Now the little one was crawling and that made everything at home much worse. They would come home from work and found him covered in dirt, crying and unable to get up. Several times he hit his head on the wall, trying to get up, even though they had covered the area with every pillow and sheet available. He was exhausted and the pills he was taking only helped him with epilepsy. They immediately ordered a wheelchair that would help him walk again and waited patiently for it to arrive! They themselves were not wealthy but they did not care for the cost. They also decided to give him antidepressants. The vet told them that they might help with his crying as it probably came mainly from the hallucinations caused by the epilepsy pills! So it happened! The next three months waiting for the stroller would be just torturous! Axl could not walk alone and his mind could not accept it. He cried constantly to get up and the poor dog stopped only when he was standing, on all fours. This did not leave much freedom for Sean and Jamie. They could no longer sleep except when Axel was asleep. They could not eat because they had to keep him upright. They could not watch TV without at least one of them sitting on the floor supporting Axl standing up! They could not even bathe if they were alone at home with the little one because he was crying and screaming like a wolf, in the slightest moment that they left him alone. They felt desperate! The wheelchair finally arrived from China and they happily picked it up and prayed that Axl could walk again. Their hearts were hurt to see him every day trying to get up and not understand why he cannot while yesterday he just could. The joy that brought the stroller to their dog and to themselves lasted unfortunately so little. Specifically two months. Axl began to lose his balance and strength in the front legs now and the wheelchair was useless without modifications, which were made, but again it was very difficult for him to walk. Axl, now 16 years grandpa, spends most of his time lying in his comfortable full with cushions bed. Recently they bought him a small plastic swimming pool where he lies on those very hot summer days! Their souls endured and their love became bigger, stronger than ever! They now know that they will do anything to protect each other. Jamie may not have stopped being afraid but she knows she is not alone. She knows that in times of trouble, her superhero, Sean, will be there for them!

That night Jamie came home and just as she was expecting, Axel was barking and 'swimming' lying on his bed, desperately trying to get up. But his Jay was there to save him. She was there to walk him in the living room. She was there to support him, as she always has been. Axl felt her tender touch and calmed down immediately. He smiled at her and with his teary eyes looked around for water. Jay ran to fetch it to him. That night the two of them slept together, quietly, after a long long time!

Parents' Sins

Poughkeepsie, 17.05.1993

The sound of the song Cocaine of J.J. Cale, covered every inch of the place. Smoke suffocatingly filled the atmosphere and in the background spread the black and white bar of the pub with all kinds of poisons. Dirty Deeds was the number one hangout at the time and if you listened to rock music and wanted to have a good time, then you would definitely go there. Men - women of all ages came to Poughkeepsie for this bar. It had of course gained a bad reputation like most of the bars back then, I guess because of the drugs and it was definitely not a place for 7-year-olds, but this particular 7-year-old really liked to wander in there. She liked the music, the Harley & Chopper motorbikes they let her ride and she also liked the fact that she made everyone laugh. Jamie was always a smart child. Witty! Funnier than most adults she has met in her life. And they believed the same, if you asked them! Dirty Deeds belonged to her parents once upon a time, up until that spring night that because of Jamie, and if not because of her but definitely with her being the cause, her parents got divorced. It was shortly after the death of her grandmother, Jamie's mother, which all this happened. One night when Jamie got up to go to the bathroom, she saw her grandmother lying on the bathroom floor. Foam was coming out of her mouth and her body was lying there motionless. Her childish mind had realized that something bad had happened and ran to her sleeping grandfather for help. Without wanting to worry him, she calmly petted his sleeping body and whispered to him until he opened his eyes. "Grandpa wake up! Something has happened to grandma!" She knew, even if she was little, what had happened. However, she chose very carefully the words she used to wake her grandfather. What followed the next days or months in Jamie's life is blank until the night her parents divorced!

Jamie's Dad "Take home your child, can't you see she is sleeping on the bar?"

Jamie's Mother "She's not just my kid, she's yours too, why don't you take her?"

The scenes that followed remained forever engraved in Jamie's mind. Voices, cigarettes, music at full blast and suddenly Jamie's Uncle, just as drunk as most of the people there, grabbed her mother by the arm and threw her to the pub's floor. Jamie, a 7-year-old child, was standing there in front of them, with her big brown eyes frightened. At that moment she hated her uncle. 34 years old now and as she thinks about it she is ashamed of that night. She is ashamed of her mother, who, obviously enraged, insulted her father on their way home, threatening to call the police and imprison him. She was ashamed of her because she poisoned her childish mind.

She tried to make her hate her father by saying horrible things about him, until she succeeded and convinced Jamie that her father was a monster! Fortunately, this lasted only for a while, because her mother's brother, who happened to be there, prevented the evil before nesting for good in the heart of his little niece. She remembers telling her "Do not be afraid and do not think ill of your father because he loves you. Your mom is angry right now and that's why she's saying all this." But soon after, she remembers her mother's hysterical words echoing on the walls of their house "Your father will come to kill us in a little while, if he comes call nine one one!" Jamie was so petrified that she couldn't think clear so she asked her mom "What do I have to dial mom?" and her mother got angrier blasting out curses "Are you completely stupid? Dial 9-1-1! You have to call the police and say my dad is killing my mom". The seven-year-old terrified Jamie nodded positively with her head while tears kept running down her numb face. She was always afraid of her mother. She had bad neurotic outbursts. Many times, Jamie invited her classmates to come home with her after school, so that her mother would not scold her for her bad grades. And there were times when, returning home, she hoped to find her father there, to avoid her mother's cuffs and explosions. When she wet her bed at night, she would wake up her dad and beg him not to tell her mom and he would caress her head, laugh and they would go together to change the sheets on the bed. That night at the bar, however, she was ashamed of him too! She blames him for letting his child follow a mother, which was obviously in a bad mental state. She is angry with her father who knew she was afraid of her mom and sent her to stay with her anyway. She is angry with him and ashamed that he did not fight in court for her custody. Her father loved her. She knew that. He was a good man and never raised his hand on her! He never yelled at her while being drunk and she never feared of him! She actually has no memory at all of her father screaming at her ever. He had a calm way of teaching her a lesson that never involved yelling or hurting. She considered him a good man, smart... wise! In Jamie's eyes her father was and still is the wisest man she has ever met! She wanted to be like him! But perhaps the fact that she finally looked like him, both in character and appearance, made her mother so angry with her, all these years. And as the years went by, Jamie realized that this might have been a little unfair to her mother. Unjust, that her mother did not want marriage but her freedom and finally got married, unjust who did not want the child in her womb but finally kept it, unjust who wanted her freedom but had now lost it, unjust to face for a lifetime in the face of her child the man who divorced her and hurt her. Jamie knew at 34 that her mother loved her in her own way, it may not have been enough for her the way she showed it to her, but she knew she tried and still tries! There were, for example, moments in history that made Jamie realize her mother's love, such as when she was an elementary school student and went to the town's only shop to pick up her school uniform. All the children bought their uniforms from that very shop. That day, the shop owner which was an old man, pushed Jamie into the store's small toilet and started stroking her thighs. The little one immediately realized the danger and managed to quickly run away to her mother! When she was told what had happened, her mother without thinking, like a raging bull, ran to the old man's shop and threatened to kill him if she saw him in front of her again! There was also this other time when little Jamie lost track of time while at a friend's house playing. Night covered the day's light and her mother was looking for her for hours! She did not scold her or hurt her when she found her, as Jamie had expected, but hugged her in relief. There was also that time that Jay turned 16 and didn't receive any gifts not even a cake. The truth was that she did not expect that stuff anyway. She was missing her father especially that day and so, alone as she was in her room, drew a birthday cake on a piece of paper. She gave the cake colored candles, wrote 'Happy Birthday Jay' and blew the fake candles making her wish! At that moment, her mother entered the room and before she could throw the painting away, her mother saw the cake and Jamie's sad face and felt deeply sad herself. Jamie disappointed her and did not want that at all. It was the same year that her mother gave her a small purple book, so small indeed that in the cover was written solely three small words. *I love you!*

The little book was about an angel and a balloon that traveled together in the infinity of time, on the high mountains and in the fluffy clouds. They were united by an imaginary red line that sometimes nearly broke, but only close enough! On the first page her mother had written...

'Jay

I LOVE YOU!

Your mom

Lucy'

"Come on" said the red balloon to the little angel.

"Come on, let's fly even higher...

In the fairy tale, in the dream, in love ...

With the transparent line of the horizon I will hold you.

Tenderly. To travel to infinity,

Always together!"*

Every time Jamie read the little purple book, her heart melted. She knew that her mother loved her. If only she had her or her little purple book, to remind that to her more often... Jamie's parents had divorced that night. The years passed and Jamie entered adolescence and came face to face with her true self. She forgave her parents for their mistakes and learned that these were the things that made her so strong! She grew up and discovered a lot about adult relationships. Among many, she discovered her sexuality! As a teenager Jay fell madly in love with a boy named Maddox and he fell madly in love with her! The two were inseparable for six whole years. Together they would learn about love and Jamie would get to know herself as a woman. She would learn that she was jealous, passionate and very erotic.

* Tania Raisi - Volanaki, I love you, IST Edition, 1998 "GREEK LETTERS"

She always liked playing with the boys in the neighborhood their kind of games instead of girly stuff, but that did not stop her from expressing herself as a woman when the time came. At 20 she would meet Sean, who would seduce her mind! Sean was the most handsome man she had ever seen in her life and the first to really make her a woman. She had never felt like this before, with no other man next to her. This would be the second time Jamie would fall in love and the last. Sean was also the only man who would break up with her and leave her without any explanation. You had no reason to break up with a girl like Jamie. She was quite beautiful, juicy as she always had extra pounds, sweet but also wild! She was a very sexy girl, fiery in bed and the fact that she was so smart made her even sexier in every boy's eyes. She only had male friends as she never got along with women. Most of them were dishonest, usually jealous of her and many times tried to hurt her out of this jealousy. They gossiped about everyone and did not keep secrets. They talked badly about their boys and were sneaky! Jamie, on the other hand, was always clear with everyone. She did not like people easily and when she did not like someone she did not even say good morning to them! She was an honest kid and never said a bad word about the boy that was next to her. After all, she had no reason to do so. All her relationships, big or small, treated her perfectly! Except, of course, from that time… that Sean left her…

The days they spent together back then in Boston were taken from a fairytale, so fascinating, so mysterious and so very erotic! She had never felt this way about anyone else, so when Sean broke up with her, Jamie experienced a deep and long depression. Sean was three years younger than Jamie, a minor while she was an adult. He was still going to school which he was trying to finish for his parent's sake; otherwise he would have already left it as he was a big bum himself. He was incredibly handsome and also incredibly addicted to drugs, something that instead of pushing Jamie away, when he told her about it, made her care even more about him. Like when he confessed to her that he was not from the USA and that he was an immigrant there. He thought she would leave him but instead Jamie loved him even more! She immediately wanted to protect him. However, her maturity and longing to bond with him so strongly frightened Sean and he left from their relationship too early. The worst thing was that he left without explanation, without saying anything to her, he just disappeared! Jamie became depressed, locked in her house for the next six months and did not speak to anyone. It was the first rejection she had felt and her body could not accept it because it simply did not know why! Maybe it was her fault that she was so in love with Sean that scared him away. They were having a wonderful time and suddenly everything disappeared as if they never existed. Any attempt to find him and talk to him was in vain. Sean avoided her and pretended she had never been in his life. This hurt her irreparably! It broke her heart and Sean had no idea how much harm he had done to her. It wasn't until much later that Jamie and Sean met by chance in Boston and started talking again. And much later that they would realize that the emotions had not simply disappeared! Every time Jamie returned to

Boston, Sean would want to see her. They would spend time together and each time they would fall in love even more. At least that's what she thought! Because there was a time when Jamie would ask Sean to be with him again and Sean, obviously under the influence of drugs, would answer her that maybe... "Maybe if you did not weight that much, maybe I would like to be with you again" and he would tear her heart in a million pieces... That was the night Jamie decided to get him out of her mind once and for all! Drugs were an integral part of Sean who seemed unable to function without them. The darkness inside him was growing fast destroying him! He had to see it! Jay returned to New York and she didn't care much anymore. She would sleep with different men and travel around the world to forget Sean. Nothing mattered though. Her soul, her mind and her heart were left behind in Boston. They still belonged to Sean.

Erotic Bond

Boston, 20.04.2014

Her heart was beating like crazy, she felt like it would explode! Her hands were sweaty and the bench she chose was very uncomfortable. She could not find a way to sit and look cool...! She felt beautiful that day. Very beautiful! Although she was not wearing anything special, a black blouse with a black short skirt, it all looked good on her, along with her blonde long hair and the beautiful foxy smile she always carried and she felt very confident about herself! She had butterflies in her stomach about seeing him again and without having to wait a minute from the moment she reached the agreed point, she saw him coming from afar riding his bicycle. He was wearing shorts and an indifferent t-shirt and had grown a beard. Just when she thought he could not look any more beautiful...! They both smiled broadly on each other!

Sean "Hello pretty face! Where have you been?! Come over here" he told her and pulled her in his big arms shaking her right & left like a doll until he finally kissed her!

Jamie "Stolen?" laughing ironically referring to his bike.

Sean "It's my father's actually. I stopped stealing stuff, I am a big boy now!" laughing.

Jamie "Yeah... I can see that!"

Seven days have passed from that day and Sean and Jamie spent every single day being together. But the time had come for Jamie to graduate, and leave Boston for good; she knew there was no other choice. Sean felt depressed at the thought of her leaving; his resentment was intense and was painted on his face. He then said to her "This time I will not let you go! Never again!" and they kissed. Jamie did not understand exactly what Sean meant. She felt more confident than ever with herself and was convinced that she would never fall in love with him again. She was playing him and she could break up at any time! The reality, as history proves to us, was very different! The relationship started again from a distance, with Jamie being on her hometown and Sean at Boston. He was twenty-five years old and Jamie was twenty-eight and it was her chance to make him hurt. To make him fall in love with her and leave him once and for all, to play with his feelings just like he had done with her in the past. The only obstacle of course was her own heart! That despite her efforts to hate him, she still loved him. She truly and utterly did! So her perfect plan to avenge him failed when she realized it and was startled by the thought. Sean had only grown up eight years after she first met him in that wretched city bar. She was twenty years old at the time and she had gone out with her friends for drinks along with her mother that had just visited her. Jamie, beautifully tanned from her summer baths in Greece, in a short black dress and very lovable, stood out in the crowd. She had just lost a bet with her friends, because she had finished her beer last, so she had to dance in front of the whole bar all by herself! She could die from embarrassment! But she never failed in something she said she would do, although she usually won the bets she placed. Slightly dizzy from the drinks, she started dancing and laughing, turning all heads in the bar. But there were two eyes that stared at her all night and were indifferent to the competition around her! Jamie after several beers and a lot of laughter ended up in the bar's toilet to refresh her makeup and the moment she was about to return to her company and just before she came out of the toilet, she would see Sean in front of her! It was the first time she saw him! He was so damn beautiful, she would think.

Sean "Hello!"

Jamie "Hello to you too!"

Sean "Were you leaving?"

Jamie "Do you have any better ideas?"

Sean "Yes! Let's play a game! "

Jamie "What game?"

Sean " Come over here… the one to pull the last paper…" he said, pointing to the paper-pulling device for wiping your hands.

Jamie "Nice! And what will happen if I win? "

Sean "You should kiss me!"

Jamie "What if I lose?"

Sean "I have to kiss you ..!"

Jamie "Fine, sounds fair! Let's play then!"

The attraction was mutual! So they started pulling the paper tissues, one after the other, without taking their eyes off each other. The tension was great between them and before the paper could finish and find out who would win and who would lose, he pulled her into his arms and started kissing her passionately! Neither of them had experienced anything like this before. His hands hugged her and his mouth was eating her insatiably and all she wanted was for this moment to never end! That same night she invited him to her house and while her mother was sleeping in the next room, he entered from the backyard as they had agreed and spent the night with her! The morning found them hugging and talking and Sean realized he had to leave before her mother woke up in the other room and found them. This was the most beautiful night of her life! This was the beginning of a karmic relationship, as history shows! No one could escape this love affair... Jamie did not know that night that she had just met her future husband!

Eight years later they would meet again and Sean would never let her go again! Four months later, the same summer, he would meet her in Corfu, a Greek island, and steal her from her company.

The Choice

Corfu, Greece, 28.08.2014

Sean appeared in front of her unexpectedly! Jamie had already arranged with her friends from the hotel to meet for drinks in the island square. But Sean was there and that changed her priorities.

Sean "Hello cutie pie!"

Jamie "What are you doing here?"

Sean "Come in, I want to show you something!"

Jamie got into the car that Sean had rented and after a short drive along the sea, they reached a small, very picturesque beach. The Ionian Sea poured in front of them majestically and a boat in the background completed the canvas they were looking at. When she noticed the camping tent that someone had set up a little further on the beach and realized that the surprise he had prepared for her was to spend the next few days together in this beach all by themselves, a smile appeared on her face! Sean had prepared everything and kept it a secret from her. He had gone to the island earlier and prepared a very romantic setting! Jamie was not a romantic girl. She was definitely rock, but not romantic! But she appreciated the scenery he prepared for her and appreciated more that in addition to the champagne and glasses that were waiting for them next to the tent, there was also a brand new toothbrush! Sean knew how much she cared for her teeth and knew that his girlfriend would appreciate this gesture. The darkness followed the day that left behind the orange fading sun that said goodbye to them and in a magical way Jamie found herself in front of another "painting"! Sean was there in front of her, kneeling and visibly anxious and next to him was a huge illuminated heart with an arrow! The heart was made of many small candles lit! Sean without holding any ring in his hands, as if it was unnecessary, proposed to her!

Sean "Will You Marry Me My Princess?"

Jamie "No no no no, please get up! Don't do it ... "she said laughing, holding her hands to her face to hide the biggest smile in the world!

Sean laughed too and got up, hugged her and continued their night. He would later explain to her that he knew that she did not believe in marriage, nor was she a religious person, and that she was also too rock to get married... but as he told her:

"You say what you want; I will steal you on my big white horse and I will marry you! I do not need your permission!
"

This statement put a smile on Jamie's face who knew that Sean was still waiting for her answer and that the first one just did not matter to him! She liked this dynamism and his determination! She liked that despite her answer and the stress he had, he did not give up and believed in them! The truth is that this was not the first time someone proposed to Jamie. She was a nice catch and burned many hearts on her way, as he was already counting three marriage proposals along with Sean's! The first was her teenage love, Maddox, who never really overcame their break up. Two years after their separation, Jamie was living with an Italian architect and Maddox kept calling her and just could not forget her. He phoned her at inappropriate times, threatened to commit suicide and he even tattooed her name on his chest on the side of his heart. The second one was Jason, fifteen years older than Jamie. She was then twenty-five years old and he was thirty-five. He was a graphic designer by profession and lived in the center of New York in a very rich house. Any girl would like to live happily in such a house! Jason and Jamie and Axel, of course, whom Jason loved so much, stayed together for almost two years. He loved Jamie very much and the truth is that despite the difficulties she stayed by his side and really tried. Jamie matured next to him like a fine wine! She went from behaving like a teenager to acting like a woman! She knew by then what she wanted from a man and from her life! So when Jason proposed to her, she simply broke up with him! Jason was smart and funny. He was neither handsome nor ugly. But you couldn't say he was beautiful, no. He was also into rock music and she liked that but he had to chase her for a long time until he finally managed to get her! Jamie had an issue with the fact that he was ten years older than her and after a lot of pressure not to think about it and a lot of chasing around, she accepted to become his girlfriend. They met through a website on the internet and Jamie had some doubts about that too! But the truth is that they fit very well together in almost everything! They agreed on the food, on the music they listened to, on the way they wanted to live, on the humor and many more. The only small problem was the alcohol. As nice the time passed when she was with him, she got so stressed and so angry not knowing if he would get home safe every night, that she could not take it anymore. Jason had an alcohol problem and would not accept it. She tried to make it work and help him out but two years were more than enough to make her understand that he will never accept it and thus never change! So naturally she had to leave him! He struggled to keep her by his side but Jamie knew that it was the right thing for her. You must first love yourself and then try to love somebody else or else chances are it won't work...

Jamie knew better and she wasn't going to stay with an alcoholic, no matter how good he was in bed, no matter how much money he had and despite the many marriage proposals he made to her. She wanted to feel proud of her choices and she certainly did not want another alcoholic in her family! The third proposal came from her Arab classmate, who in their brief relationship decided that she was the woman of his life and wanted to take her with him to Lebanon and marry her, and finally, we come to Sean, who had grown up since the last time. Who had turned into a real man now! Sean who knew what he wanted and was not afraid to claim it. Sean who, when he was told that she would never take him seriously if he did not quit the drugs, he simply quit them! No questions asked! Sean who made the conscious decision to choose Jamie over everything. Sean who fell madly in love with and who chooses to love to this very day. For better or for worse! To the worse that would come, like that night, that he will never get out of his mind!

Six months later, Jamie wrote a letter, on five papyrus pages, of how she felt about Sean and mailed it to him. They maintained their relationship from a distance. She covered the beautiful pages with her intoxicating perfume and decorated the envelope with red and black silk ribbons! Finally she sealed the crimson envelope with her gold stamp that had her initials on, which she had bought years ago in Rome and sent it to her lover. She was certain of her choice! She informed him that when the file arrives in Boston they would open their cameras in order for her to be able to see him read it for the first time. She wanted, as she told him, to see his reactions and she did not want the distance that separated them to deprive her of this joy! The file arrived and Sean opened his web camera. Jamie was on the other side of the screen, looking at him impatiently and listening to him read the pages she had written a few days before. She remembers Sean blushing from his anxiety reading Elytis' monogram, a Greek love poem that Jamie had discovered during her travels in Greece, and in fractions of time she saw him tearing! His beautiful eyes glistened with tears streaming down his face as he read Jamie's answer to a question he had asked her six months earlier that summer!

«I will marry you! »

Sean "You make me the happiest man in the world!" he told her and wiped away the tears of joy!

And she would really do it!

Daring Thoughts

The pain was unbearable! Tears ran down her face and wet her hair, blurring her vision. With bare feet she ran to the balcony of their apartment and grabbed the railings that prevented her from being found in the vacuum. Her mind was playing ugly images and the voice in her head was telling her to do it. She knew there was no reason to do so. But she wanted to play with the idea! To feel what it is like to flirt with death. She could not stand their quarrels. She did not want to argue but she knew that she was a difficult person. Demanding! Tough in her decisions when she was angry and did not compromise with anything less than the perfect for her! The apartment was located on the fifth floor. The railings were icy for April but her feet were not cold. She knew he would see her and maybe that's why she did it. She heard the door open behind her and knew Sean was home. He had returned from their little fight and he just wanted to hug her. It had been only ten minutes since he opened the door to leave the house and he had already regretted it. So he returned and entering their bedroom, he saw the blue curtain waving from the air. The balcony door was open and through the transparency of the curtain, Sean saw Jamie on the balcony. Jamie ran one foot over the railing. He went crazy! He ran to her and she pulled her leg in again. She wanted to see her like that. She didn't care about anything. She did not know the reason she put herself in this situation but it did not matter. Her soul ached and no one understood her. No one understood the sadness she felt deep inside, so intensely that sometimes she felt her whole body ache. But mostly she felt pain in her heart. No matter if she had everything, no matter if she knew that, no matter how much Sean adored her and carried all her favors. Jamie was happy, really happy, except for those days, which came at an unsuspecting time, without warning and without a specific reason and darkened her soul. Obviously there was a problem. She was aware of it. Sean knew it too, and if he hadn't understood it well by then, he truly felt it that night. Raw! As a problem always should be managed, with all its truth, naked, as it had to be seen. Jamie saw fear painted on Sean's face. As he pulled her into his arms to protect her, he made it very clear that he did not want to see her like that again. That there was no reason for him to make such desperate moves because he simply loves her! He would leave the house if she did something similar again, he clarified it to her! That move scared him for good!

Sean "You have everything and we love you, what else do you want ?!"

Jamie "I want to stop feeling. Make the pain go away, please, I can't take it anymore." she told him in a trembling voice as she cried incessantly.

Sean hugged her so tightly that she gasped. He had shown her many times that he cared. That he loves her like crazy and that he is not going to leave her life again, as he did at the age of seventeen. He was trying to understand the darkness he saw in her eyes, but he did not know that you shouldn't be trying to understand the darkness, but to illuminate it... to see what is hidden inside it. That night Jamie got scared too. She was afraid she would lose him. She was afraid that she too would be lost. Seven months later, the pain returned. The idea of taking her own life was screaming in her mind. She opened her laptop and typed *'depression what are the signs'*. It was there in front of her, seven out of ten. That same night, the quarrel that followed with Sean when he returned from work, for something insignificant as always, but which ignited her anger and with the already bad psychology that she had the previous days, made her explode! It made her explode like a strong chemical reaction and the shock wave that came from this explosion spread chaos around her. The speed of the fragments was so high that whatever safety distance you kept at that moment, nothing could save you. Jamie was scary. And the next minute was not scary at all; Sean would find her locked in the bathroom cutting off her hand with one of the fragments. Breaking the door, he found himself holding her hand. He removed the glass she used so comfortably as if she were cutting crafts for schoolwork and began to take care of it. Jamie, such an optimistic girl, full of experiences and knowledge, degrees and travels, strong and so smart. Now she was lying on the cold floor of her bathroom, crying, so very vulnerable!

Jamie "please, make it pass, please, make it pass, please, make it pass, please..." she mumbled, continuing to repeat it over and over again.

Sean "Which my love? What you got? Tell me what to do?"

Jamie "Please, let it pass; make the pain go away. I cannot take it anymore."

Sean hugged her even tighter in his arms. He felt bad. He felt helpless. He also wanted to banish pain. Only he did not know how; he did not know if such a thing was even possible! That night they both slept as if they had no worries on their minds. They were so psychologically tired that day that the only way to leave it behind them once and for all was to sleep deeply. Until the next night, when the nightmares would begin!

New York, 30.04.2017

Sean woke up to the screams of Jamie next to him who had not yet woken up. She was fighting with the sheets and the demons in the nightmare she was seeing and her sweat had soaked the mattress in their bed. Sean tried to calm her down and then with a sharp breath the screams stopped, her eyes opened and tears began to flow down her cheeks. It was the umpteenth time this month that she had nightmares. Intense, scary and so vivid nightmares. Jamie needed several hours during the day to recover from these dreams. It had been two years since she first started seeing them and the frequency with which they now came to her sleep was frightening! She was afraid to sleep and cried at the thought of what he might see again. Sean was anxious to see her suffer like this and not being able to do anything to stop them. He said he understood her but how could he? How could he understand what it is like to be robbed of your sleep for two whole years? How could he feel what it is like to be afraid to close your eyes at night? How could he understand what it is like to see every night one after the other many times in a row, to die? How could he understand the stress and horror that these nightmares were causing Jamie and depriving her of the right to just live a carefree day?! Of course he could not. Sean did not know the whole truth about these nightmares. Jamie kept the details secret. She did not tell him that he was the one who chased her every night that he was trapping her and he was scaring her so much. How Sean's hands gripped her neck and squeezed it so hard that she died out! Sean was the cause of her death every night with all the possible and improbable scenarios. The environment in the nightmares was constantly changing, once was in their first home and the next was on another planet. Amid ruined cities and the destruction of civilizations, the killer remained the same. And that was Sean. A few months later, that summer and a few days before their wedding in September, Sean found Jamie in the sea. It was four o'clock in the morning and the waves were splashing on the rocks of their favorite beach. Petali, a small paradise far away from the bright lights of New York, hidden between two green Greek mountains, hosted them for second summer. Sean and Jamie loved camping. Jamie loved Greece very much and distinguished her among all the trips she had made. That's how Sean loved her. That August the heat was unbearable, but the three of them had a wonderful time. Axel swam with his little brown legs with the help of the propeller he had for a tail, in the deep blue waters and then rolled on the white pebbles that covered the entire beach. He was happy and so were Sean and Jamie. In the mornings, before the sun set on their beach, they would dive into the icy waters just few meters away from their tent. Jamie would sunbathe and Sean would solve the crossword puzzles he had brought with him. At noon the heat was unbearable and they rarely got out of the water. They played with their inflatable mattresses and laughed with their souls. Sean and Jamie fit in very well as a couple. They constantly played together like little children and were just as competitive with each other. They were also very much in love! Summers always felt more in love than ever! In the afternoons they would relax in the only tavern that the beach had and they would talk to the local owners. Every night they lit a fire in front of their tent and cooked the meat that broke Axl's nose, which made him go crazy, dancing in front of them, begging almost for a bite from Sean's well-cooked chicken. Overlooking the moon in their tent, they would make love every night and the two of them would sleep or crouch around the half-extinguished fire until dawn. Sean fell into the sea with rapid movements reaching her in the water. Her clothes were wet and her eyes were fixed on the crimson August moon. Then he remembered what she used to say to him.

Jamie "This moon is mean. The August moon is the most dangerous, don't laugh Sean," she said trying not to laugh herself.

Sean "Oh really?! So what makes it so dangerous? "

Jamie "Most murders happen on days like this! The bloody moon drives people crazy, changes them! I'm telling you its mean." Her eyes were weeping. Red like the moon.

Jamie "You have to promise me you will burn me. When I die Sean I want you to burn me like a Viking! Put me in a boat and set me on fire with a flaming bow from afar. "I do not want to be buried and be eaten by worms."

Sean "What happened to you baby? How did you get into the water? Let's go out, you'll catch a cold! How long have you been in here?"

Jamie "Promise it!"

Sean "I promise... let's go now!"

Jamie took off her wet white T-shirt without taking her eyes off him. Her wet huge breasts appeared and her hard nipples waited for Sean's mouth to suck them. Her hair was soaking wet and fell on her shoulders and before she knew it she had sunk to the dark bottom in front of his feet. He felt her pull his boxer shorts into the water and her mouth furiously take his penis sucking it, which before he even realized what was happening, it had already become hard! With his strong, tattooed hands, which Jamie loved so much, he pulled her out of the water and began kissing her with his fleshy mouth, eating every part of her face. He grabbed her two big breasts, which drove him as crazy as any man, and began to bite them insatiably. He was at her mercy! Jamie's groans testified her hellish thirst to feel his penis deep inside her and with that in her mind she was whispering to him...

Jamie "I want you inside me ... fuck me please!"

Sean "Shhh... no! I want you to suffer a little more..."

Jamie bit his lips hard as she felt his finger slide inside her. Sean was even more irritated as he felt Jamie's fluids and without being able to wait any longer, he turned her around. His hands grabbed her hair and pulled her head back. "I want to finish inside you..." he told her and grabbed her rich round ass. Jamie shuddered at this risky phrase and leaning forward a little brought her hands back, asking him to grab them and got ready to be devoured! Sean went inside her and stayed there for a while holding her tightly on top of him. His penis was about to explode and Jamie felt it throbbing inside her. She liked his penis. It was long and thick and fit perfectly in her pussy. Trying to hold on so it wouldn't end so quickly, he started coming in and out slowly. But her groans in combination with the ability of this woman to fuck his mind and his body at the same time, the words she said to him and her hot breath in his ear, all this, was beyond his power and he finally lost control! He then grabbed her and started fucking her hard! He fucked her as if it was their first time or even better as if he had never fucked a woman in his life before. The feeling they both had every time they made love or sex was so unexpectedly intense and insatiable. Jamie shivered in his arms as she felt him in every cell of her body. Sean, ready to finish, heard her ejaculate as his penis pierced her mercilessly and suddenly his fluids spilled inside of her. Two minutes later, while they were done, Sean was still inside her. The moon was constantly looking down on them.

Guilty Past

Police were knocking on Mrs. Magnolia's door. The sixty-three-year-old lady recognized them through the curtains. With slow steps, as she had just left the operating room, she got up to open the door wondering what the policemen were asking on her home.

Mrs. Magnolia "Good morning! How could I help you officers? " She said in her sweet reassuring voice.

Policeman " Where is your granddaughter Mrs. Magnolia? We are truly sorry to bother you but something happened to your neighbors and we… would like to see if the little one has seen or knows anything."

Mrs. Magnolia "But of course, just a minute. I would swear I just heard her coming in. JAMIE, baby, come here my love. "

Jamie, thirteen years old girl, appeared in front of her grandmother wearing her favorite sneakers full of dirt from the alleys she used to play. Her shorts looked worn and her knees as usual scratched from playing games with the neighborhood boys and the trees she was constantly climbing and injuring herself. Her cheeks were flushed and her beautiful brown hair cut too short for a girl.

Policeman "Hello doll. Do not be afraid we will not keep you long from your game. We want to ask you a couple questions. "

Jamie stood motionless in front of them, looking them in the eye, without showing a trace of fear. "Ok" she said with such stolidity!

Policeman "Do you know who wrote these insults on Mrs. Beatrice's wall?" he said pointing from where he was standing, right across the house, a few feet beyond theirs.

Jamie "No, I do not know"

Policeman "Someone saw you and your friend Susan painting the wall late last night."

Jamie "Yes we did but we are not to blame."

Jamie's grandmother went out in the courtyard of her house and looked at the neighbor's wall. On the white wall, painted in bright orange letters, were written: 'Stella and Stacey are sluts.' Grandma Magnolia's face was instantly turned red with shame!

Policeman "Why did you do that?"

Jamie "I had no choice, Andersen's son threatened to kill me. He put the knife he carries on my neck and told me that if I did not write it he would kill me. He had just been released from prison; what is stopping him from going back?"

The policemen were astonished and frowned. They said thank you and took a step to the right to leave. It was clear that their next stop would be the house of the bully former prisoner, when Jamie realized that and stopped them. She told the whole truth, that the whole thing was her idea, she did it and persuaded her friend to follow her and that Stella and Stacey were really whores! She said all this with one breath and without any obvious regrets. Ms. Magnolia hugged Jamie and informed the Policemen that her grandfather would paint the wall and Jamie would apologize to everyone. Jamie apologized to everyone as she should, but did not apologize to Stella and Stacey no matter how hard people tried to convince her to do so. That summer Jamie would break a very expensive wooden door of their other neighbor with an axe and no one would ever find out. Her little stumbling with the insults on the wall taught her to use her mind better. To think more thoroughly about her steps and not to put herself and most importantly her grandmother in the same position again. She would be hunted down by angry car drivers and truckers passing by the highway, because she would throw stones at them with her sling and steal from a younger girl in her neighborhood a bracelet given to her by her dead mother. But she would feel bad for that bracelet that before she could return it back to its holder, she lost it and was punished by her own self very harsh indeed that summer. Jamie, mainly out of great shame, did not leave her grandmother's house at all that summer to play in the streets with her friends. She knew she was considered a thief and had to be punished. So she stayed inside and the only time she went out was to go with her grandfather to the stable, to take care of the cows, the pigs and their ducks.

Jamie, like most teenage children, was a little naughty. Or we could agree that maybe Jamie was a little wilder than the other kids. Maybe she stole stuff more often or maybe she got involved in more quarrels than the others did. Jamie was a cheeky child as she grew up and was no older than ten years old when she was caught taking off a boys' pants. Of course, she did not take off their pants, she just ordered them to do it and they did it so willingly! Jamie was much younger than these boys and yet they obeyed her! She has always had a more developed sexual curiosity compared to children her age. This may have been due to some images that inadvertently pierced her childhood mind.

San Juan, Puerto Rico, August 6, 1996

That summer Jamie would be staying with her mother who decided to go on holiday to San Juan. San Juan is the capital of Puerto Rico, a small island in the Caribbean Sea. Jamie did not want to go with her mother and her mother's friend Larry, to an island in the Caribbean or anywhere actually. She wanted to stay with Grandma Magnolia in Poughkeepsie and spend the summer with her friends. Who would ask a ten year old child what she wants to do?! Thus began their journey. After a five-hour flight from New York, they landed in Venezuela and from there in a small boat from the port of Caracas they finally reached the green San Juan. The beaches of the island were enchanting! Palm trees and flowers were spreading almost everywhere your eye fell. There were also many parrots on the island that seemed to be familiar with the people around them. Jamie went crazy with the parrots and had set a goal to hold them all in her hands. She made friends with some stray dogs, since from a young age she had a special love for dogs, but she also found children of her age with whom she spent a lot of time together! She rarely saw her mother during the holidays, nor their friend Larry, and usually if she needed anything, she would find them drinking at a bar.

With her new friends, Jamie hung out on the island square, playing and running everywhere, stealing chips and ice cream from the kiosks and sneaking into San Juan's only summer cinema, through the back door and without a ticket every night, until they were caught and kicked out of course. In the evenings they gathered again in the square and the locals told her the myths of their island but also the scary stories with the ghosts that haunt their beautiful place. So in San Juan, Jamie had her first childhood love and her first kiss. The little boy was a year younger than her and his name was Chris. Chris held Jamie by the hand and proudly took her home to his mother, who welcomed them and offered them delicious homemade sandwiches with sauce and meat, a traditional recipe. Jamie had never eaten something so delicious before! Thirty-four years old today and she still remembers and seeks the taste of that sandwich. So every night, Chris and his friends accompanied Jamie to a nearby hotel where they were renting a room. Jamie did not care that she was wandering to the island alone at night, nor that her mother did not look for her and did not drug her along with her. She liked that she had her freedom! Which child does not like this?! But she was still ten years old and anyway, she should not be wandering alone in a foreign place, unaccompanied. One of these afternoons that she was once again left alone, she was returning to their hotel, when she saw her mother in the arms of a stranger. Her feet just stopped and her eyes were already remorseful that they looked in that direction. She froze as she watched them kiss like lovers. It was really scary for Jamie! It was the first time she saw such a scene and she was ashamed to see her mother in this role. They immediately noticed her standing a few meters away from the window that separated them and they panicked. Then Jamie cried as she heard her mother angrily shouting at her to go to their room. The days that followed were painful for Jamie, as she was forced to be next to her mother and next to this stranger who was so unexpectedly kind to her and pretend that everything was fine. Jamie felt punished. Her mother was constantly angry and forced her to spend time with the foreigner's daughters. She herself preferred to stay locked in their room at the hotel, until this carnival was over and they returned home to Poughkeepsie. Leaving San Juan behind, she made her promise not to mention any of this to her father... And so she did. Jamie did not tell anyone about that trip. She did not even want to talk about the parrots and the friends he made in San Juan. As if she had not felt the joy at all during this holiday. It was as if she felt the joy and then someone stole it from her. So she chose to forget.

Today a mature woman, Jamie, having felt the erotic desire herself, recognizes her mother's behavior as something normal. Something that in the eyes of childlike innocence seems monstrous comes adult empathy and absolutely justifies it! The way Jamie grew up was a bit unorthodox, but there is no way she would change that today! She loves her parents and although she would change some bad moments, she certainly would not change them with anything! She knows that in the year 86 ' that she was brought to life and raised through the smoke and music and the bars, the rock mentality was in the forefront and affected every aspect of their lives. It was in the songs, in the places where she was growing up, in the way of thinking, in the sex and definitely in the way they would eventually raise her! Rock mentality defined her. She had formed, along with many others, her own mindset and that would not change either. She made her what she is today and she feels proud to wear that skin.

Omens of Death

New York, 24.07.2020

Jamie opened her eyes and looked at the glass in front of her. As she poured the last drops of iced Coca-Cola into her glass, she leaned over to cool off her face as the drops jumped on the ice cubes. The heat that day was unbearable, she thought. The thermometer they had at the hotel reception showed 103F but it was definitely much hotter than that. You could hardly breathe in that heat and the small fan on her feet no longer made any difference. As she stared at the ice cubes in her glass with great dedication, her mind went to Romania and her eyes that were forcibly kept open, finally closed again, allowing her to be drawn into her dreamy imagination! So she immersed herself in her thoughts and in the journey she had made during the first year of their relationship with Sean. The image of Romania, a frozen country with a severe winter, tried to drop the temperature on Jamie's body. Her mind wandered again to the icy stone alleys of the village of Brasov, with its picturesque shops and warm wooden boarding houses. As a child, her dream was to visit the castle of Dracula at some point and she made it happen. The journey from Bulgaria that they had visited first, by train to Bucharest of Romania was fascinating! They had booked a large bunk bed, just for them, and for hours they gaze at the snowy landscape from the Carpathian Mountains, which unfolded dramatically in front of their window! Their trip to Bucharest was Sean and Jamie's best trip. Embraced, they walked the streets of Romania and played with the three meters of snow that covered everything! They tasted the local flavors and bought a lot of Romanian chocolates and souvenirs for everyone back home. They had traveled all over Bucharest and visited the village Brasov where the castle of Count Dracula was located. They went to every museum and monument in the area, they had even explored the thousands of small casinos that popped up everywhere on their way in which they made also a small profit! In the evenings they would discover a different restaurant or a bar and get drunk with their love. Then they returned to their hotel 'George and the Dragon' and made love in their marble bathroom! They stayed in Bucharest until New Year's Eve, which they found spectacular! All the residents of Bucharest had gathered together along with the tourists, in front of the Romanian political palace and were watching the show that had been prepared for them. Famous singers were invited and with the 3, 2, 1... Fireworks exploded over their heads high in the sky! Then Jamie made the wish to stay together forever and live happily ever after... and she was so sure that the stars would grant her wish that night. The fireworks lasted around forty minutes and all this time Sean was looking at Jamie and Jamie at Sean as if there were no thousands of people around them. They felt like staring in their own movie and the end was predicted to be extremely happy! That same night, Sean gave her a wooden ring he made himself from the arbor, at the entrance of their hotel. Jamie was flying in the clouds!

The sirens of the patrol cars and the desperate cries of the people outside in the streets violently interrupted her thoughts. She immediately ran to see what was happening when she saw the corpse of a young woman and gasped. Frightened, she quickly took her eyes off this image and soon discovered that she could not but only look back. The lifeless body of the twenty-five-year-old was lying frozen as the asphalt was watered by the girl's deep red blood. The crowd gathered more and more around the corpse, full of curiosity and as soon as they saw the horrible spectacle, they turned their heads away. Some were screaming and someone more sensitive, unable to bear the harsh image, vomited in a corner. Jamie caught herself getting used to the blood in front of her pretty quickly you would say. She returned to the hotel, remembering that she was still working, and walked behind the reception desk to her post.

Her shift was still in its beginning and that meant she had six hours ahead of her. Her thoughts were concentrated in the blood of the young girl who painted the curb and thought that inanimate body could be hers. That night, on the balcony of their house, that Sean got so frightened. If she had done it, how much would her absence cost him? How long would it take him to rebuild his life? Would this image ever leave his mind or would it destroy him once and for all? Jamie clouded over these thoughts. She looked up at the antique wooden clock, which stood majestically in front of the reception, and looked at the time. No way! She shouted from within! The clock hands showed twenty-two forty! How time passed so quickly without her realizing it, her mind could not comprehend it. She was probably absorbed in her thoughts more than she should have been. Now she was afraid that a customer had passed by and she was sleeping upright. What an embarrassment! Nah, she would have listened to them if that was the case, she thought and at that moment her colleague came in to get her out of her misery. That night she dreamed of the young girl falling from the ninth floor of the building and recognized her clothes. The red cotton blouse she was wearing this time was Jamie's favorite. The girl's skinny jeans looked a lot like hers and her face would swear she saw... Jamie woke up to her tangible screams and saw Sean holding her hands and shaking her!

Sean "Baby what did you see? Calm down! You saw a bad dream shhh! " Jamie burst into tears.

Sean "I was trying to wake you up for three or four minutes. It was impossible. You scared me! Did you see the girl? " Sean looked quite anxious. He took her in his arms and hugged her tightly. Jamie fell asleep right away.

The next day, Jamie went at the hotel. She worked again an afternoon shift as usual, because it is extremely difficult for her to wake up in the morning. Apart from the nightmares and the night sweats that were more frequent lately, in the mornings she had dizziness and intense nausea. She always blamed it on the fact that she is not a morning type and that she slept late at night, so her body could not cope with waking up in the morning!

Arriving at the hotel, at 32 Emerald Street, her eyes fell on the alley a little further, where last afternoon the young girl landed from the 9th floor of the newly built building from where she fell. From the entrance of the hotel when she got there, she could see the staff all gathered together sitting on the leather sofa in the background were three policemen were talking to the management. Entering, Laura, the fifty-three-year-old maid, ran to catch up with her. She said they were ordered to leave their posts immediately and gather here. The police wanted to take a statement from them about the girl who committed suicide yesterday.

Jamie "But we do not know if it was suicide."

Laura "Do you think she was killed?"

Jamie "I'm not saying anything; she is just too beautiful and young to be wanting to end her life so quickly. And what do they want from us? How could we know what happened, we did not even know her!"

Laura "They want to ask us where we were at that time and if any of us had seen or heard anything from the building that she fell. You see, from our upper floors, you have a very good view of the opposite building. People reasonably ask! Someone may have seen her as she was about to jump."

Jamie "Yes, or her killer!"

The discussion was interrupted by the eighty-three-year-old owner, who, despite her advanced age, her dark shiny hair stood so elegantly caught up high on her head. Next to her stood one of the policemen, who was terribly annoyed by the smoke coming out of Mrs. Orwell's long silver pipe and so he took a step forward and introduced himself to the hotel staff. In the end, the policeman who was actually a chief inspector after he was properly introduced himself to them and put things in their place, regarding the title he held, he assured them that he would not bother them much. So it happened. One by one, alphabetically and per section, they gave a statement and returned to their post. Jamie was last questioned and after she explained to them that she could not see or hear anything, since from the reception where she worked you cannot see the floors of that building at all, they let her return relatively quickly, behind the Reception. But in her attempt to get up from the comfortable sofa she was sitting on, got dizzy and collapsed on the marble floor. The marble, deep green in color with gray waters was brought from the Mediterranean by Mrs. Orwell's great-grandfather as she often used to tell them. The hotel was in their family for many generations and like the antique wooden clock was invaluable to Mrs. Orwell Maxine.

Jamie opened her eyes and saw in front of her, her eighty-three-year-old boss talking intensely to a gentleman dressed in blue. This charming stranger wore glasses and a surgical mask hung from one of his ears. He put his hand on Mrs. Orwell's shoulder and after he left in a hurry.

Mrs. Orwell "Did you wake up my sweetheart?"

Jamie "Mrs. Maxim, what happened? Are we in the hospital? "

Mrs. Orwell "My poor child, you don't remember anything? One moment you were talking to the inspector and the next you were lying on the floor. You fainted. "

Jamie "Sean, I need to call him..."

Mrs. Orwell: "Calm down, my dear, we have already informed him and he should be on his way."

Jamie "Did the doctors tell you anything? How long have we been here? "

Mrs. Orwell "They won't say anything to me Jamie, they said they would talk to you as soon as you woke up. Give me a minute to call your doctor."

Jamie was right about the doctor after all. Up close he was even more handsome. But his gaze was sullen and cold. He raised his eyes and looked at her. He could not maintain his serious look and staring into her eyes he finally bent and smiled!

Doctor "How is our patient doing?" and caressed her hair gently.

New York, 06.05.2021

Jamie put some of her clothes in a pink backpack without being too careful not to wrinkle them. She put enough and as soon as the bag was full, she sat down on her bed and waited. The dizziness was now unbearable and even this small chore, tired her. She heard the door slam shut and Sean appeared in front of her.

Sean "You cannot travel alone, do you understand that? You'll drive me crazy! Do you think your parents would want you to travel in your situation and all alone?"

Jamie "You don't understand that I have to do it? I miss my grandparents and my dad; I have two years to see him! I have to go. I will be fine! I will go first from Poughkeepsie and then I will return to New York to take the plane to Germany. I've booked my tickets. You do not need to come and pick me up from the train station; I have arranged a taxi to take me to the airport. When I return in two weeks, I look forward to seeing your face and Axl's, waiting for me at Arrivals! She said and threw herself with all the force she had left in his arms.

Sean "I don't want to quarrel with you on your birthday. Tonight we will go out to celebrate. Where does my little girl wants to go?"

Jamie "Amusement Park please kind sir! And after we can go for a pint at Molly's, let's eat those nice bratwursts and chat. I have something important to tell you!"

The next morning, Sean took her to Grand Central Station to take the train to Poughkeepsie. His gaze had changed. He looked scared and nervous. It was not so much the trip to Germany that Jamie wanted to do on her own, but what she asked him to do for her last night...

Jamie had just returned from her trip to Germany. The heat had made its presence felt in the heart of New York City and they were already wearing their summer clothes. Jamie felt burning from the inside out and made sure to cool little Axl quite often, who was now watching her cook with his brown eyes. The heat rising from the pot simmering the ragout was torture, but she wanted to cook for them today no question about it. Tonight they would eat on the patio which was the coolest place in the house. The ragout flooded their home with smells and next in turn was the polenta, grandmother Magnolia's recipe. They would accompany their meal with a green rocket salad with baby carrots that that morning had taken fresh from the planters of their garden! Of course, the red wine would not be missing from the table, which they would finally open as they had forgotten how many years it had been in their possession. There was no reason to hold it anymore he thought. The little radio that Jamie used to listen to while cooking was now playing Elvis Presley's Can't help falling in love, when Sean popped up at the door. He had just returned from work and without her noticing him, she felt his hands on her hips caressing her. A smile appeared on her face and she asked him to dance with her. He couldn't say no to her and after he threw his work bag on a chair he hugged her and so they danced. Jamie's face was perched on his neck and her lips kissed him gently. Her hands were holding him tight and she could feel his heart beating. Tears welled up in his face that he could no longer restrain.

Jamie pulled herself away from his arms and now her fingers were wiping Sean's wet cheeks.

Jamie "Baby, don't think about it. You are very strong Sean. You have to be strong, for both of us. My God, how much I love you! " she said and threw herself into his arms again kissing him. The music had just stopped and her place took the today's headlines.

'The fall of the young twenty-five-year-old woman in Madison Square was a brutal murder. Her fiancé took her life by throwing her from the building on Emerald Street that afternoon. Almost a year later, the police finally closes the case. '

Sean stared at Jamie as if he had committed the crime himself. She seemed just as worried. Then Jamie smiled reassuringly and pulled him close to her.

Jamie "I'm not afraid baby! Neither should you. We love each other... don't forget it! In this, in the previous and in the next life! I want you to be strong now that I'm not. She said and kissed him on the forehead.

Summer wine was now playing on the radio and Jamie loved that song.

"Strawberries cherries and an angel's kiss in spring"

My summer wine is really made from all these things,

Take off your silver spurs and help me pass the time...

And I will give to you, summer wine

With eyes fixed on his, she sang the song and gently bit her lips. With two movements, Sean took out his 'spurs', as the lyrics of the song suggested, and pulled her closer to him. The ragout was still simmering and the polenta would have to wait…

May left and was replaced by the even warmer June. Jamie would take her summer vacation and the sick leave and Sean arranged to also take his summer leave and maybe more. This summer they would travel around the world! Their savings were enough to go to the places they wanted all these years and end up in their favorite, Greece! It was all planned and in three days a life dream would come true.

That same night, Jamie woke up from a conversation. The man who was heard was not shouting at all, he was just whispering, one could say. But even that noise was enough to wake her up. After all, lately her sleep lasted only little, as she often woke up with the slightest sound and even more often she suffered from nausea. Jamie sat up in her bed and then headed for the sound that woke her up. The voice of the man who had been talking on the phone for so long was becoming clearer and clearer. Arriving outside Sean's office, she noticed that the door was ajar. She might not have woken up if he had closed it.

Sean "Will it be a problem? I want you to reassure me." His voice was not as sure as other times. Jamie noticed a concern in the way he talked to the person on the other end of the line.

Sean "And she will not feel anything right? No pain at all? This is the most important thing. It must not hurt at all. " She wondered who was the person of interest. What was her husband talking about?

Sean "I have to close, I hear something. As we said on August 28, I will wait for him. Thank you my friend." The last phrase was said in Greek.

The sound of the chair being pulled back scared her. She opened the door and stepped inside the room. Sean had not noticed her and he was now lying on the desk, with his both hands supporting the head he was holding bent.

Jamie "Sean... baby? Who were you talking to?"

Sean "I did not want to wake you up, sorry, with no one. I have ordered a package from abroad and it is seven hours behind. So they thought it was a good idea to ring me up early in the morning. Go to sleep, my beauty, I will also come in a little while."

Jamie noticed that Sean's eyes were wet and the vein in his forehead was throbbing as he spoke. She did not want to pressure him anymore so she said nothing and went back to her bed. Old Axel was waiting for her there, welcoming her every time waving his tail! The last months, Jamie can't get enough sleeping with him, as she constantly wants to feel him next to her. To hear his heart beating and his breathing that soothingly lullabies her! This way she feels safe and Axl feels that he is still protecting her! Like back then in Boston when the two of them were studying and every friend of Jamie's was under scrutiny by her little friend, who sometimes growled and rushed and sometimes greeted them by wagging his tail vigorously and licking their hands as a sign of sympathy. So Jamie knew very well who to trust and who to keep away from her! Axel not only protected her from humans but also from other animals and his height or size never stood in the way! He was a brave dog and he was not afraid of anything! Just like his boss, who would never let anyone mess with him! Immediately, came to her mind one of their worst moments in history. Once upon a time outside the university, they were attacked by a tall and husky white dog. His teeth were yellow and pointed; saliva was dripping constantly while he did not stop grunting until he attacked them! Without thinking about her safety, Jamie bent down and lifted Axl up to protect him while he did not stop barking and attacking the white stray dog that was now within breathing distance of them. Even when she lifted him higher, almost above her head, making a great effort to keep him there, Axl did not stop barking and wanted to attack their formidable enemy. The white dog with one movement got up on both his legs and rushed to Jamie, barking to leave poor Axl from her arms to confront him. Axl could not stand a chance! He was so small and the other one was too big. His two legs were now resting on her chest and his saliva was running on her blouse and she had never been more frightened in her life! Jamie started shouting for help and a passerby who happened to hear her, went to them and immediately started shouting for help too; wishing someone else could hear them as the sight of the white huge dog attacking them, was too scary to take it upon himself! The stranger started shouting at Jamie to let Axl down and run away to save herself and another pedestrian who had just arrived at the scene, told her to do the same. They even tried to convince her that if she let Axl down, the white dog would calm down and not hurt him and so she knew she was alone. She managed to shout that she will not let Axl out of her arms and that she prefers to be eaten alive rather than to put him down, when the white dog lowered his legs from Jamie's chest and slowly began to step back, grunting, without losing eye contact from Axl, who was still hanging over Jamie's head! The stray dog shook its hind legs on the standing grass, howled for a moment like wolves do and abandoned its prey. Jamie was still holding Axl high, feeling her arms clasped in the same position and her heart still beating like crazy! She abruptly lowered Axl into her arms and held him tight there without taking a step. The people around were talking to her but she could not tell what they were saying to her, probably out of shock! She thought about how much she loved that dog in her arms and did not expect anyone to understand her. She also knew that the white big dog felt this love, respected it and fled. That day God noticed from above how much they love each other and protected them, that was it, she thought! Jamie lay down on the bed, hugged him and after kissing him on the head and muzzle several times, they fell asleep together.

Sean huffed heavily and fell on his desk, hitting his head three times. Then he sighed and looked at the computer screen to his right. A list of some strange words unfolded in front of him. The names were in Latin.

Conium Maculatum

Aconitum Napellus

Atropa Belladonna

Amanita Falloides

Nerium Oleander

Ricinus Communis

Colchicum Byzantinum

Hyoscyamus Niger

Taxus Baccata

His eyes were fixed on two of those words for a long time.

Mandragora Autumnalis. He grabbed the crystal bottle with the golden liquid it contained, behind the bookcase and poured the content into his glass. The ice cubes in it had melted for a while now, but did not seem to bother him. With one sip he drunk all of it and filled the glass again. He whispered "Mandragoras Autumnalis" and his eyes watered again. Tears ran down his chin, which was now resting on the desk. Sean burst into tears.

Dreamy Kykeon

Two days later they were traveling to Peru. Their great journey had begun. In Peru they would climb the lush Machu Picchu, admire the Inca finds worshiping the Sun God and take endless photographs of Lake Titicaca. There they would ride the boats built by Peruvians and Bolivians, with totora reeds and be enchanted by the representations of the old traditions of the Inca empire on the island of Amadi. Next stop, the tropical island of Kauai in Hawaii. There, they drank the most beautiful cocktails of their lives and ate traditional coconut pudding that the locals offered them with such a smile! They walked along the coast to Anahola beach and kissed under every palm tree they encountered on their way. Sean and Jamie fell in love with the carefree nature of that land and promised that in their next life they would both live in that place! The next few days on the island it rained, so they gathered at their favorite Tiki Bar and danced to Hawaiian rhythms wearing Lei around their necks! Lei, locals called the colorful traditional garlands that the little girls made with the exotic flowers of the island. Jamie wanted to take one with her as they were leaving, even though the flowers would wither; she wanted to keep that memory a little longer.

To Dublin, she had been many years ago, but could not find anything that has changed. She visited the beautiful library of Trinity College which she did not have the opportunity to see on her first trip there and after renting a car they set off for the famous coastline of Ireland, ending after many picturesque lighthouses and beautiful medieval castles, which they met on their way, to Galway. There they walked the cobbled streets of the city, as the car was really useless at that point, and found a room in a small guesthouse that seemed to be taken out from an Irish fairy tale! The entire hostel was covered with climbing green ivy and the only entrance was a small wooden carved gate, quite low in height, as if dwarfs were living inside. The whole scene reminded Sean and Jamie of the movie 'The Hobbit' that for one whole summer they were watching it on their computer almost every night! Not because they liked it so much, but because they did not have access to Wi-Fi and so they spent the entire summer watching the same movie over and over again. So now, every time they meet it on TV, they laugh at each other saying 'Aha! Here is a nice movie we have not seen yet!!! 'and then they sit on their couch hugged and watch it, guessing what the characters will say next and betting on what was going to happen in the next scenes! Bets that of course they both won, but alternately, just to make it more interesting! In Galway, they noticed that the streets were full of musicians, writers, and other artists, and most of them spoke the local Gaelic dialect. Jamie thought that if they walked the same streets hundreds of years ago, then everything would be even more interesting as the residents and artists on the streets would be dressed in vintage clothes, which she adored so much! Of course most of the people around them would wear rags because there was great poverty in the past, as history testifies, however, they would have the opportunity to see carriages pulled by stately horses, they would see how the original recipe for their favorite Shepherd's Pie first started and they even might had been able to see the Celtic kingdoms ruled by kings as they were seeing in the movies and if they were lucky enough, they would have the opportunity to be invited to one of the royal festivals, where singers, storytellers and jesters would entertain them all night! Jamie was enchanted as she thought about all this! At that moment her grandfather came to her mind. He was also a storyteller and a great poet! He painted several paintings, some of which hung in her paternal home; He was a nurse and one of the best football players in one of the most famous teams of his time. But above all, he was the best grandfather a little girl could have! Every night, he would go to Jamie's room and tell her stories until she quietly fell asleep. Grandpa Willem was Irish and had been in love with his wife since he was a child. Therefore, it made a lot of sense for Jamie to think that the reason he died in the end, was the loss of the love of his life, of Grandma Jennifer. A few years after her death, Grandpa Willem could not bear his life without her and so he abandoned completely any try to stay alive. He did not take his medication, he stopped eating, he drank more than he could handle and so the old storyteller left this life behind him happy that he would meet his great love once again! At his grave Jamie had placed the medal she had won at her school volleyball games along with a commendation from the play she had staged and played that year, a tribute to both an artist and a great athlete, both of which accompanied a letter...

'To Grandpa Willem! The best poet, painter and footballer I had the honor of him being my grandfather! I love you! Your granddaughter Jamie ...'

Night had fallen and darkness covered most of Galway's streets when Sean and Jamie decided to enter the guesthouse they had found, which with a blackboard at the entrance, informed strangers that rooms were available for the night. Passing that low portico through the heavy wooden door, Sean and Jamie felt entering another dimension! Live music was heard the moment they stepped inside and in the background you could see the band in their traditional costumes playing in folk rhythms, entertaining the people at the tables in front of them that seemed to be having a good time. To their left was a huge stone fireplace and they had never seen before such a big one that almost touched the ceiling. At the base of the fireplace, the hosts had placed large wooden elves that looked so real and the tavern windows were upholstered in handmade red curtains filled with green clovers. A tray passed quickly in front of them and managed to enchant them with the smells of the goodies it carried... The sweet potatoes, pies and well-cooked meat had just stolen the show making Sean and Jamie realize how hungry they were! There was plenty of wine and beer on the tables and seemed so inviting when a hand landed hard on Sean's shoulder.

Stranger "Welcome folks! What can I do for you? I am Joone, the owner of the tavern and of the pension." he said with a cheerful and welcoming style.

Jamie "Good evening! We need a room for tonight and the sign outside said there was vacancy."

Stranger "Well, if it was written, it must be true beautiful! Come here, let me give you your key and then I am waiting for you in our tavern to quench your thirst!

I want you to tell me how you got to our little Galway! You are Americans right? "

Sean "Yes Americans... of course we will come! Give us five minutes to leave our bags and prepare three cold beers, Mr. Joone! "

Mr. Joone "I like you boy!" he said laughing out loud "two floors above you are, the one with the golden door and the frog, number 13"

Jamie "Thank you very much!" they said strangely and set off for their room.

The corridors were spiral and full of family pictures. There were so many frames that you wondered how many generations of Irish people went through this guest house. At the end of the corridor, on the second floor, there was actually a wooden door painted with gold shiny paint and its knob was a green frog. Just as Mr. Joone had told them. Jamie was thrilled as a toddler! They spent the rest of the night with Mr. Joone's family, laughing and dancing and after they ate and drank sweet homemade wine, made by

Joone himself which made them smile even in their sleep ... they started for the very small but very welcoming room! The next morning the two travelers ate again at the pension's graphic tavern, only now the place for the guest's breakfast under the light of the strong summer sun, looked completely different from the previous night. The smells however, that came from the food on the tables were just as fragrant and intoxicating! Freshly baked bagels, sausages, beans and potatoes, eggs cooked in three different ways for all tastes, bacon and jams, homemade breads and sweet and savory pies were just a few of the options on the huge buffet of this small B n B. Sean and Jamie left that morning after greeting the Joone family members one by one, taking with them a small piece of their hospitable guest house.

Next stop on their journey, the city of the thousand minarets! Or else, Cairo! Viziers, sultans, harems and mummies, you were waiting for them to pop up in every alley of Cairo's bustling and mysterious market, also known as Al Khalili. The market was the first place Sean and Jamie chose to discover and the smile of excitement painted on their faces accompanied them throughout their trip to Egypt! Al Khalili was taken out of a Hollywood movie. Hundreds of shops crammed into the cobbled streets of the market, promising you an unforgettable walk. Oriental lanterns hung left and right as you passed through the alleys and were sold almost everywhere. Gold-plated jewelry and pure silk scarves were worth only a few Egyptian lyres compared to other Western cultures and the smell of spices permeated with the smell of narghile and that of the tea, as you passed by outside the small cafes. Jamie was excited! Sean too was thrilled, only you could understand that something was bothering him, when his smile was cut short by bad thoughts. But the truth was that he also didn't want this journey to end! And what wouldn't he give for it to never end! His thoughts, this time, were interrupted by a gypsy, who fell on him as they were searching the shop with the handmade wooden camels, which they had passed few minutes ago.

Sean "Are you okay lady?" Sorry I did not see you there! "

The old gypsy opened her eyes wide and slowly raised her two trembling hands caressing Sean's two white cheeks. Next to the woman was a young girl, probably her granddaughter. Sean laughed awkwardly and pulled back when the gypsy held him tight and approached his face.

Gypsy "Only brave, you can say the action you will do... Your pain will grow my boy and you will not forget no matter how hard you try. »

The little gypsy was translating into broken English while the older one was talking and suddenly stopped when her gaze met Jamie's surprised face. Her hands left Sean's frightened face dangling to hold Jamie's hands this time.

Gypsy "This life you've lived was short for you my dear. You are not done yet, my little one, he will find you again in the next one. " and wiped the tear that escaped Jamie's eyes that she had been trying in vain for so long to hold back. The old gypsy then grabbed the hand of her little follower and they turned in the opposite direction to leave. Shortly before she left, however, she turned back and looked at Jamie.

Gypsy "He will always find you!"

Sean and Jamie looked at each other and turned to look at the gypsy lady who was now gone. The lively days in Cairo were lived intensely and adventurously while the magical Arabian nights were spent at an inn in the city center where Sean and Jamie were pretending to star in a movie or they were laying in the luxurious open-air bar of their hotel overlooking the stars! In the mornings they were getting up before the darkness subsided and went for a walk in the desert on camels, while one night they even left the comfort of their five star hotel and spent it with a Bedouin family, literally under the starry sky of Egypt! They visited the ancient city of Memphis and admired the Sphinx, while from the awe they felt when they found themselves in front of the pyramids they forgot and did not take a single photo, so they visited them again the next day! They strolled with a felucca in the murky waters of the legendary Nile River and that same night the owner of the luxury hotel where they were staying, had them invited to his suite to watch his exotic harem dance the famous oriental belly dance! There they were fed fresh and dried dates and drunk lots of local beer. Sean was ecstatic with their savory food and especially with the lamb in the hull that was marinated with herbs and spices while Jamie, who has a special love for sweets, tried almost everything! Basbousa and Ais al Saraya, Lokmet el Kandi with which Sean fed her in the mouth, Asura and her favorite Um Ali, a rich dessert made from puff pastry, milk, cream and nuts, and in a way reminded her of the Greek bougatsa she ate on summers in the islands. Jamie like another Sehrazad and Sean like the crazy Sultan, lived their own thousand and one nights, unfolding a different tale every night, trying to live… the dream a little more! But as big a dream seems to our mind, it is only a few minutes long in reality or only seconds. Just so quickly they felt that their trip to Egypt was over and they did not want to pack their bags this time…

The next morning found them flying. Sean and Jamie were looking down on Egypt saying goodbye and which magically disappeared when their plane passed through a thick cloud. Sean kissed her on the cheek and his face became serious when the pilot announced their destination.

Greece, Athens, 14.08.2021

The plane landed in the capital of the neighboring country after three and a half hours of flight. Sean and Jamie headed to the counter with the rental cars, after first picking up their suitcases and setting off by road for Mount Dirphys in Evia. The little paradise beach called Petali, was located behind Dirphys mountain which whoever crosses it feels closer to God! With an altitude of over 1,700 meters, its peaks and many times its roads are lost in the clouds scaring the foreigners who visit it for the first time! Sean and Jamie were crossing Dirphys for the third time and were now aware of the dangerous points on the mountain and the sudden changes in the weather. Even in the summer they encountered many times intense storms and heavy rainfall, while other times you could even see snowfall! This time Dirphys welcomed them with a cool breeze, while sun's golden rays pierced her white plump clouds. Jamie was staring out of the car window, sticking her head out, taking deep breaths of fresh air when the car suddenly stopped! Right in front of them was a beautiful mythical creature and it was staring at them without a trace of fear! A deer stood haughtily, blocking the narrow road, waiting for them one might have said. Sean looked at Jamie who had already gotten out of the car.

Sean "Baby, where are you going?! This is a wild creature; it is not a farm animal. Be careful not to scare it because it might attack you!"

The deer seemed to be much larger than usual and especially more beautiful! Its hair was smooth and shiny as if someone was combing it every day and its eyes were shining! Its horns were brown gold, although Jamie would swear it was pure gold! With slow steps she approached this magnificent animal which did not step back, only kept looking at her. Sean got out of the car and got ready in case the animal, despite its calmness, chose to attack them even though nowhere in history had they heard of deer attacking humans. The deer with the slightest movement usually flees. It is its survival instinct and its speed along with its horns is its weapon against other predators. Jamie has always had a good relationship with animals of all kinds. From an early age, she spent more time with the animals on her grandfather Liam's farm than with her friends! She watered the hens with the hose and searched their nests for fresh eggs, fed the pigs with yarmas which was animal food mainly made of barley and played with them in the mud, although her grandfather tried to scare her by telling her that they are dangerous animals and might eat her if they get the chance… She cleaned the fur of her favorite cows and she polished it with a wire brush and finally she stole her grandfather's crook and pottered around on the mountains with the goats and sheep. Poor grandpa Liam, although he was a tough man, shook his heart every time he lost sight of little Jamie, who kept finding her in a different place each time. One afternoon he was so frightened that he called her parents, fearing that he had lost her for good. So after searching the whole stable, bit by bit, without being able to find Jamie, he called her parents, who arrived at the farm panicked. Scared as they all were, they started looking here and there when after about twenty minutes, Jamie's father finally found her! Jamie had fallen asleep under a bull! With slow movements they pulled her from under him and when she finally woke up from the shake, they scolded her for good. She was told that this bull is dangerous and her grandfather even he barely approaches him, so they have him alone and tied up, because once the huge animal had even attacked Mr. Liam! Unable to justify their anger, Jamie replied that the bull is her friend and that he lets her pet him and that there is no reason to be afraid of him because she plays with him every day! She also told them that it is the most beautiful animal on the farm and that she wants him as a pet in their house in the city!

Jamie "What a beautiful divine creature you are?! What are you doing here, waiting for us? Will you let me pet you? " she said talking to the majestic animal in front of her. Jamie spoke softly to the deer in a sweet and calming tone, hoping to let her get close enough. When she reached two steps away from the animal, she stopped and spread her arms in front of him, lowering her gaze thus declaring submission. The deer then sniffed the air in front of her and immediately took a step forward, thus approaching Jamie a little further. She reached out to touch it and tears rolled down her excited eyes. A shiver went through her body when she felt his heart beating and she looked it in the eyes. Her hands now caressed his beautifully sculpted horns and the deer took another step forward. Jamie rested her cheek on his muzzle and then kissed it on the nose. What she was living that moment was unreal! Sean was filming the whole scene with his phone and he couldn't believe his eyes either. Jamie hugged the deer with all her might and thanked it for the gift it gave her. The deer then took two steps back and bent one of its legs while lowering its beautiful head in front of her! Jamie looked at Sean in surprise, who was just as surprised as she was. She got up and before she could do anything else, the deer left galloping through the tufts of white clouds that stretched in front of them and made the scene even more magical! Sean and Jamie got back in the car without exchanging a word, feeling so many things at once but mostly feeling endless joy and gratitude. Sean turned the key in the car when drops began to fall on the car window and within seconds the weather changed, breaking out in heavy rain. Sean and Jamie looked at each other and burst out laughing! Eight hundred meters away, the weather changed again to summer and the clouds receded as they began to lose altitude, allowing the deep blue of the sea to be seen from afar. Their personal paradise was a few minutes drive away.

Arriving in Petali, they realized that they were not alone. Although summer was coming to an end, there were still several campers on the beach. Sean searched with his eyes for the place where they had been camping for the past two years and when he found it empty he was relieved. They immediately started carrying and setting up the tent and in less than half an hour the basics were already over. Jamie camped in the mountains and seas from an early age and her father taught her how to light fires, throw knives in the trees, fish with rods, but above all he taught her to always respect the nature. Her husband Sean was introduced to the camper's life when he met Jamie, so he had no choice but to love it himself! From the very first years they were together and traveling, they rarely stayed in hotels and preferred life in the campsite. They had camped in places like Plymouth Rock in Wisconsin, at the Estrella campsite in Barcelona overlooking the Iberian Sea, they had even camped in London, Lee Valley, when they visited it for an AC / DC rock concert. They were last seen camping with a Bedouin family in the White Desert of Egypt and this is the third time they have set up camp in Greece, specifically in Petali. The next morning, they woke up to the sounds of drums and wind instruments. The music seemed to be traveling from behind the mountain, where the village was located and reached their ears as a welcoming sound! The same afternoon, after enjoying the icy sea, they got dressed and left for the small village with the music still in the background. As they found out arriving in the village square, August 15, was a great religious holiday for them as well as for the whole country! The Virgin Mary was celebrating and this explained why the bells of the church above their beach did not stop ringing that day. The Greeks are famous for their hospitality, so the locals welcomed them warmly confirming their good reputation and with the few English they knew as most of them were quite old, they informed them that in the evening a big celebration would take place and that they should stay and celebrate with them! So it happened! Jamie and Sean located a small picturesque tavern overlooking the sea and very close to the square where the festivities would soon begin. They ordered local red sweet wine to accompany the mezedes* that soon appeared on their table that was constantly full and Mr. Christos who brought them used to grab Sean and Jamie by the shoulder and tell them 'eat up my children go on!'. On the table were first-class delicacies such as fresh fish, which Mr. Christos himself fished early in the morning with his boat, anchovies, delicious cod and a wonderful cold fish salad called tsirosalata, that Jamie had to say the word many times to pronounce it correctly. The classic and not exceptional village salad, which is one of the first foods you learn coming to Greece, Sean's favorite grilled

*Mezedes plr, mezes sngl, is a Greek word meaning various treats in small dishes that usually accompany local drinks in typical Greek taverns.

goat cheese called saganaki and of course zucchini fried in batter with the famous tzatziki and plenty of sourdough bread made by Mrs. Maria, Mr. Christos's wife! The live music did not stop for a moment and just before dark lay upon them, the people had already gathered around the plane tree in the square and hand in hand they started dancing! Jamie, who had been "hit" for good by the drunkenness of the sweet wine making her cheeks slightly pinker, got up from the table and took Mrs. Maria by the hand following the others in the dancing circle and tried to learn the pace of the dance, which made her feel so alive at that moment. Sean was watching her from their table, enchanted. He was looking at her rose cheeks and the sweet wonderful smile that won him over from their very first acquaintance. He looked at her long blond hair waving on her shoulders and the tattoo on her leg up which made in Boston when they met, and he looked at her eyes that shone like the deer they had encountered on the mountain as they came. He would swear at that moment that they were exactly the same! Jamie was now looking at him laughing and inviting him to dance with her. He wiped the sweat from the heat on his cheeks and ran next to her. That night in their tent, under the moonlight and the music of the sea popping up in the sand, they made love and stayed awake until dawn, looking out of their tent window at the starry sky! The next few days passed quietly on their small beach that they had now been left alone. The campers had returned to their cities and their jobs, and the only sounds that could be heard now were the bell ringing every Sunday from the church and the sea waves. That Sunday however, the sound of the bell was different and a little later they understood why! From their beach you could see the churchyard that was now decorated by some locals with white, yellow and purple flowers and everyone who arrived was beautifully dressed and smiled. After about an hour and a half of waiting, the bride appeared! The wedding dress she wore was not white but blue and white flowers adorned her black short hair. Jamie thought of her own wedding dress which was also light blue in a vintage line with a large blue bow sitting in the middle of her waist. She had been searching hard to find something she liked when she and Sean decided to get married and when she saw the blue dress in the shop window she rushed inside to buy it. She did not want to wear white because she did not believe in customs but also in religion and for this reason they did not get married in a church but in the town hall. The light blue vintage dress she saw in the shop window was her favorite color and exactly what she was looking for in her wedding dress and even the fact that it was a little small and did not button did not stop her from buying it! With two small modifications, the dress sat perfectly on Jamie and from the remaining fabric she made a bow tie for Axl that of course could not be missing from the wedding! Their parents though, were missing because they decided to steal each other and so they never experienced the party of a big wedding. They were little interested, however, because they could have the party and the family gathering at any time in the future. Or was that no longer an option? Jamie wondered. The bell started ringing again and Jamie woke up from her thoughts. She lifted her head from Sean's chest where she was leaning and shook him to open his eyes.

Jamie "Tomorrow I want to go to the big village, to the post office; I would like to send some postcards to my family."

Sean "Yes, let's go, I wanted also to tell you, I have to meet an old friend who is passing by the area and I told him that we are here. Do not worry I will not be long in coming. By the time you get to the little bookstore you like, I'll have already finished." he said, stroking her head.

Jamie "Oh yes, I can't wait for it! Do you think Mr. Oliver is alive? How old should he be now? Yes baby I will be waiting for you there, I hope he has new stories to tell me. Do you think he will remember me? Three years have passed... »

Sean "There's no way he's forgotten such a dummy face, no matter how old he is." Jamie was already attacking him and hitting him in the head biting his nose like she always did when they were playing like this. Sean grabbed her and started tickling her, something that drove her crazy and she did everything to escape but in vain. Jamie kept laughing by the tickling hitting with her feet the hot sand when Sean stopped abruptly and pulled.

Sean "What have I done? I'm such an idiot! Are you OK baby?" his face was frightened and immediately Jamie's laughter stopped.

Jamie "What happened? Why did you stop? I'm fine..."

Sean was now looking at her bloodied T-shirt and Jamie did not understand what had just happened. Sean took off his shirt and put it on Jamie's nose which did not stop dripping. When she finally felt the blood slip in her throat, she realized what had happened.

Jamie "That's why your acting like that?" she said laughing at him. "It's just a little blood baby, don't freak out!"

Sean "Stop laughing just STOP! I CAN'T DO THAT ANYMORE, DO YOU UNDERSTAND? I CAN'T BEAR WHAT YOU ASK OF ME TO DO, I can't pretend in everything, as if nothing is happening!" Sean burst into tears and fell into the arms of Jamie who stopped laughing and with both her hands held him tightly on her chest up. She held him like babies are held during lullabies. That's how Sean felt at that moment, small and vulnerable. Jamie had never seen him like that before, she was scared, but did not show it.

The next morning Sean got up earlier than usual and left the tent. The day had just begun succeeding the night and the sun had not yet reached their small beach. Like every other morning, Sean started for his walk in the small forest behind their beach, to gather wood. For some days now, he was preparing this wooden boat, something like a raft, which could barely fit two people. Today would be the day to finally finish it. An hour later he returned to their tent and realized Jamie had opened her eyes and was looking for him. He also noticed how empty and deserted the beach seemed with only these two there and that under other circumstances he could stay there forever.

Jamie   "Where have you been? I woke up and you weren't next to me."

Sean "Good morning beautiful, I had gone to the forest to gather wood for the fire. Why did you wake up so early?"

Jamie "Nightmares ... and you picked it up?"

Sean "Pick up what?"

Jamie "The wood, did you pick it up?"

Sean "Oh no, I left it there; I thought you were calling me, as if I heard your voice and so I came back. I will take them later. Get ready now to leave for the village. "

Jamie wore her favorite summer dress, the straw hat that she could not remember exactly how she found in her things and her sandals and started for the post office. Despite the early hour, the village was already full of people, among whom you could see several tourists. In the village there were also many who decided to live there after visiting it as ordinary tourists and instead have made it their home, such as for example the Oriental Hermione with her spices, the baker from Albania, Mr. and Mrs. Smith who left Manchester and the boring office work for good and retired and Mr. Oliver the village bookseller, also English and Jamie's favorite person! Sean left Jamie in the village square and he went to the cafe a few meters below, grabbed a small table overlooking the endless blue of the Aegean and waited for the friend he was to meet. Jamie headed to the small post office in the village and went inside. She took four closed envelopes out of her bag and went to the counter. She asked for stamps for abroad and started sticking them in the envelopes. One envelope was for her grandparents, the other was for her father in Germany, another was for her mother in Poughkeepsie and the last envelope, hermetically sealed, the word 'FRAGILE' was written in the center in red letters and above right, Sean Bales, New York, 10023, West 75th Street. Jamie paid for the stamps and went out. She looked around and when she was sure she was alone, she quickly dropped the letters in the yellow mailbox and headed for Mr. Oliver's bookstore, two blocks away from where she was. The bookstore was exactly as she remembered it three years ago, nothing had changed. The dark green color of its bricks on the outside had faded slightly from the sun and its brown wooden door was frayed, most probably from the saltiness brought by the wind from the sea, but otherwise it was exactly as she remembered it! His shop window was, as always, filled with old and modern books from around the world, and the dust that covered them instead of pushing you away added a little more mystery, making the little green bookstore particularly appealing to Jamie, who was now sitting and staring from outside. The glass of the shop window was painted, by Mr. Oliver himself, with a special color for glass and depicted a green tree deeply rooted. Behind the tree now appeared the figure of old Oliver trying to climb the staircase, while holding several books in his hands. The doorbell rang and Jamie appeared in front of him smiling.

Jamie "Good morning!"

Mr. Oliver "I will be right with you miss. Just give me two minutes. " he said, slowly descending the steps of the iron staircase, trying not to drop the books he was holding.

Jamie " Hello Mr. Oliver, do you remember me?"

The old man took off the glasses he was wearing and replaced them with another pair hanging around his neck. His face lit up and his wrinkled blue eyes moved.

Mr. Oliver "By the Gods of Olympus, I'm afraid my eyes play tricks on me! Is it you Jamie dear? Oh! It is you my precious... come here, let me hug you. »

Mr. Oliver's Greek was at a very good level, but of course he preferred to speak his mother language whenever conditions allowed. He had come to Greece a few years ago and fell in love with Mrs. Ismini, a local beautiful and delicate lady that Sean and Jamie managed to meet the first year they visited Petali. That same year, Mr. Oliver lost his beloved, who left quietly while she slept, one winter night. Since then, Mr. Oliver has never been the same person and kept himself in his books. He was a kind man and a sweet figure with a warm smile and the locals accepted him from the first moment he stepped foot in their small village and took care of him to this very day.

Jamie "Mr. Oliver, how are you? How glad I am to see you healthy! How much I missed this little paradise you have created here! Tell me your news and show me please your new hidden diamonds... I can't wait! " she said full of excitement seeing her old friend!

Jamie hugged him tightly as she hugged her grandfather and then they sat in his old and equally dusty with the rest of the place, office. Old Oliver lit the red porcelain lamp that was placed on a stack of books and grabbed her hands. He asked her how her husband Sean was and where he was, how their life was going in America and what Axl her beloved dog was doing. He confessed to her that it is difficult to live alone without the smile of Mrs. Ismini and that many times he even talks to her for endless hours and that he is very close in getting the reputation of the madman in the village. They laughed a lot together and dusted off some really remarkable books he was holding to give her if he ever saw her again! Jamie told him about all the joys in her life and also the reason they came this year to Evia island. She opened her heart to him for the hardships she was suffering and confessed her dark secret. Mr. Oliver's eyes filled with tears as he felt Jamie like a daughter and sank into grief. His mind could not hold it! The entrance bell rang again and a familiar voice shook them and they got up from the desk.

Sean "Is anyone here?"

Mr. Oliver "Shaun my boy! Come here, it has been ages. »

Sean «How good to see you Mr. Oliver! It's been a long time for sure… What did you do with my beautiful wife? »

Jamie appeared from the corner holding with difficulty about a dozen books in her hands.

Jamie "Look my love, he kept them for me, we'll take those back home with us. It is unbelievable that he found them, look, this is the original and this was left by a stranger in the cafe, quite a rare book... first edition!»

Sean "But yes... of course... we will take them with us." he said frowning unable to say anything different.

The three of them sat down and told each other their latest news, while Mr. Oliver's mind was anxiously constantly thinking about the conversation they had previously had with Jamie. Everyone's faces became serious and silent when the sound of the doorbell interrupted them again. Two Dutch tourists had heard of Mr. Oliver's shop and came in like excited little bookworms ready to explore it! Jamie and Sean cordially said goodbye to their old friend. Mr. Oliver wiped Jamie's wet eyes and kissed her on the forehead.

Mr. Oliver "Be strong my dear! As I met you so stay. Strong! Thank you for not forgetting me, my wife always liked you and Sean of course. Be strong!" he said, drowning out his last sentence out of emotion. Jamie, visibly upset, walked out of her favorite bookstore and wiped away her tears, which did not stop running down her face. Sean had stayed behind and as he left he stood at the door.

Mr. Oliver "Shaun ma boy... just one second my dear!" he picked up a small leather-bound book from the shelf behind him and handed it to him, whispering in Greek...

« Να είστε εγκρατείς να είστε άγρυπνοι.

Γιατί ο αντίδικός σας ο διάβολος, σαν λέων που ωρύεται,

Sean glared at him and nodded. He took the book from his hands and left with his head bowed, but before closing the door behind him he stopped again and turned to look at Mr. Oliver one more time.

Sean "I love her you know! I really love her. "

The door behind him closed and the familiar bell rang again, shattering the bubble over the head of Mr. Oliver who dared to look back for a moment, marking the end of a story as he knew it. That night they returned to their tent and Jamie wanted to dive into the sea for a night swim to cool off. Sean would go and gather wood for their fire and then bake the sausages they took that afternoon from the village's butcher. The sea that sunset was pure enjoyment! The water hugged gently her body that felt burning from the inside out and as naked as she was, seduced the moon that was looking at her and she left herself in the saltiness of the sea that once again won tonight! The night completely covered their beach and only their camp fire could be seen from afar. Jamie swam ashore and the fire grew bigger as she approached their tent. Her eyes searched for Sean but in vain. She came out of the sea and shook her hair, wiped herself with the towel and quickly got dressed by the fire as she already felt cold. The warmth of the flame soon touched her face and the glass of wine she poured for herself felt like medicine that moment. She looked up at the sky and noticed how clear tonight was and full of stars that illuminated the mountain tops around their beach. The moon was full and red like every year in late August and scary as Jamie used to tell Sean every time. Its light made the church bell shine in the dark and two figures appeared in the courtyard. The figures looked like men and one was wearing something on his head, maybe a hat. As her eyes got used to the distance and the darkness, the second figure reminded her more and more of Sean, until she was sure. It was him! She could recognize him anywhere. Jamie froze in her seat. What did he do at such a time and meet a stranger in the night? Why didn't he say anything to her? Maybe she shouldn't have known, Sean never hid anything from her, maybe it was a surprise. Now the stranger in the hat reached out to Sean, giving him something in his hands. Sean grabbed it and processed it and then put it in his backpack. They talked for another two minutes and then the stranger got into a van and disappeared. The fire in front of her was flickering and Jamie grabbed a stick and shook it to rekindle it.

Sean "Oh! Did I come just on time?! The coals are done, time for sausages!" he said, as he left from his hands a stack of wood that he seemed to have cut earlier.

Sean "And then we'll light it again and it'll burn all night for my baby!"

Sean grabbed Jamie and kissed her and drank some wine from her glass.

Jamie "Where have you been? I was scared when I came out and I did not see you."

Sean "Yes, I had a hard time finding wood for our fire in the darkness. But I was not so late, my little complainer! "

Jamie smiled at him and drank the rest of the wine from her glass.

Jamie "Do you want some? It's perfect! I want to get drunk tonight...»

Sean "I'm going to take off these shorts and put on my pants, it is quite cold today. Watch out the sausages and the fire and I'm coming with more summer wine! Something tells me I have to watch out for you tonight... »he smiled at her and left for the tent.

Jamie "Or should I be the one watching you...?" she whispered to herself and out of the corner of her eye she watched Sean change in their camping tent. Sean took out of his bag an object wrapped in cloth, from what Jamie could see, looked at it and put it back in, closing the bag tightly. Then he changed his clothes, grabbed the wine of Mr. Christos and ran next to Jamie.

Mandrake

Petali, Greece, 28.08.2021

That morning he woke up with a knot around his neck. The sun hadn't yet shed its light on their small beach but he already felt like something bad had happened. He turned right to hug Jamie who was sleeping next to him and realized that she was not there. His heart started beating faster and faster and his pulse escalated as he came out of the tent and anxiously started looking for Jamie! But she was nowhere to be found! He searched in panic the beach running here and there and when he couldn't find her, he started yelling her name with all his might! Less than five minutes later, Jamie appeared behind him.

Jamie "Sean? What happened?"

Sean "Where have you been?" I woke up and I did not find you, I was scared! " he said and fell in front of her on his knees. He was very upset and you could see it just by looking at his face. His eyes were red and the vein of his face was shown, betraying the intensity of his body. Jamie now lowered herself in front of him and her knees touched the sand. She grabbed his face with both her hands and kissed him on the forehead.

Jamie "Good morning grumpy!"

Sean smiled.

Jamie "Maybe you should get used to my absence sweetie. I will not be by your side forever, you know. You have to be strong, that's what we said! " she said with a smile and kissed his eyes. Sean hid his head in her chest and hugged her.

Jamie "Get up baby, today is our last day; I want to do so many things! I want to spend it with you! "

Sean "Can we go to church for a while?"

Jamie "In church? But what to do there? " she said laughing out loud as she, like Sean, did not believe in the Church. As they did not believe in Christianity and in any religion basically. But they believed in God! Or Allah, or Krishna, or Buddha or whatever you want to call the deity. They believed in him, whatever his name was. "Ok let's go, if you want." and started for the chapel high on the hill.

The church was deserted but its door was open to the faithful, so they were able to enter at any time. Jamie thought she had a long time since she last visited a church and the last time it must have been when she was afraid they would lose Axel, their dog. She remembers being so frightened that entering a temple and seeking the aid of Christ, was according to her heart the best thing to do at that moment. So she agreed to follow her husband to that church, without even asking any questions. Sean lit three candles and then sat in a chair and prayed. Jamie sat right next to him and held his hand. She prayed for him from within. She wished for him to find peace. Suddenly the lights came on and the sound of the wooden door was heard from behind them. Jamie turned and saw a priest coming in.

Priest "Good morning my children, I am Father Athanasios. How are you child? Are you ready?"

Sean "Good morning Father."

Jamie "Ready for what Sean?"

Sean "Are you ready to remarry Jamie?" he told her with a smile and knelt in front of her. In his hands he held the same wooden ring that he had made for her in Romania at the time, from the arbor of their hotel.

Jamie "Are you crazy?! Again?"

Sean "Crazy for you and YES again !!!" he put the ring on her finger and ran his hand through the hair falling on her face.

Jamie "Yes Sean, I'll marry you! In this, in the previous and in the next life! The answer will always be one! Yes! "

Sean "I will always find you; be sure!" and grabbed her to kiss her. Father Athanasios had already put on his vest and was preparing for the Mystery, when voices began to be heard outside the church and became louder as the time passed. Jamie opened the church doors and then she saw them! People from the village all dressed up, holding flowers and bags with rice. Among them stood out Mr. Christos and his wife Maria, the girl from the post office of the village along with her boyfriend, Sean's red-haired friend who he knew from a young age and finally stayed for their wedding and of course first row, their friend Mr. Oliver, wearing a bow tie and a tall black hat that stood there moved smiling at her.

Mr. Oliver "Sean asked me to accompany you. I don't know how the idea sounds to you my dear; I might as well not do it my sweet Jamie." Said to her looking somehow shyly.

Jamie hugged him with tears in her eyes and grabbed him by the arm.

Jamie "It would be my honor, Mr. Oliver. I would be an honor!"

Sean "Thank you all for coming and filling this beautiful day with smiles. You are all really wonderful! Forgive me now, I have to get married! "

The audience laughed and followed them inside the church which was now fully lit. Father Athanasios stood there waiting for them, ready to marry them in the presence of the Father, the Son and the Holy Spirit. So it happened! Jamie and Sean may not have understood much of what was happening and what Father was saying in Greek, but they did not really care. Today was the twenty-eighth of August and like today some years ago Sean had proposed to her! The wedding had been ratified for the second time and the couple emerged from the church door holding the flowers given to them by those in present. The churchyard was transformed very fast into a dancing floor for the couple's first dance and a table with grills and appetizers had already been set up as if by magic! Ten tables were placed in front of the buffet that could just fit the guests and the happy couple. Jamie could not believe her eyes! Maybe that was what Sean was secretly preparing last night. At that moment she thought how much she missed her parents and grandparents but most of all Axl her faithful dog who had accompanied her to their wedding on the first time.

Jamie "I miss our family, you know; I always said that if we did that again, they would all be with us. I miss Axl! "

Sean "I imagined you would miss them, that's why I invited them today..."

Sean pulled the cell phone he had open behind his back and showed it to Jamie. They were all there looking at them! All together behind a camera that little Axl was now licking! Her joy was indescribable! In a block on the top left was her father deeply moved, below him was his brother with Jamie's grandparents who were wearing their good clothes and Grandma Magnolia forcibly holding her tears, in the next square were Sean's parents with his sister's newborn baby and in the center her step father with her mother Lucy who were holding her beloved Axel! They were all there! Jamie sent them kisses and told her father how much she wished he was there to escort her. But he told them he had the next best man, Mr. Oliver! He told them that he loved them. He loved them all. Jamie cried and Sean hugged her for their first dance! The people around them fell silent and Elvis' voice was heard through the church speakers.

'Like a river flows,

Surely to the sea,

Darling so it goes,

Some things are meant to be.

Take my hand, take my whole life too....

Cause I can't help, falling in love with you...!'

Jamie sank into his arms and forgot everything. She forgot the world around her. She forgot that her parents were still watching them on camera. Sean was her whole world. She was so lucky to have him, to love her so much. So completely and indefinitely. It made it so easy for her to adore him all these years! Their day was spent with the most relaxing way, with Sean and Jamie enjoying their swim in the turquoise waters of their exotic beach. Jamie felt so full of love and was so grateful for her life. Joy had flooded her brain, which made her now incapable of seeing Sean's real face! His eyes were black as if he was thinking something dark and his movements were very nervous. His face had changed and if happiness did not stop her, she would see it herself. The light of day was lost and the two of them gathered in front of the tent. Tonight the fire was quite large and the flames were flying in the air as if attacking invisible birds and quickly went out disappearing in the dark sky. Sean and Jamie had to sit far enough away to avoid the aggressive flames. The full August moon had made its appearance over their beach and would keep them company like every other night, so tonight.

Jamie "Hold me tighter look how scary it is. As if it laughs ironically, as if preparing to do something bad. I told you this moon is mean. Beautiful... but dark! "

Sean "Come on baby, we all know we cannot see the dark side of the moon," he said teasingly.

Jamie "Invisible you mean. No we can't, not from where we are. Its dark side though, you might... if you try; it does not deceive me. " she said gloomily and perched on Sean's lap whose heart was now beating like crazy!

The night passed with Jamie narrating various mystery stories she had known since childhood and with Sean hugging her and kissing her constantly. Sean kept throwing wood to their fire which was alive all this time and shortly before midnight he announced that he had bought a very special herb for her to drink, from the mountains of this place. Sean pulled a few coals out of the fire and placed on them an old copper pot they had to heat their water. He added fresh water to the kettle and then removed a plant from his bag and held it ostentatiously in front of Jamie.

Jamie "What is this?"

Sean "This, my dear is a Mandrake. Mandragoras Autumnalis! "

 Among the green broad leaves of the plant there were dozens of purple flowers while the large and fleshy root of the plant hung below it. The most special feature of the plant was this root. It looked like an anthropomorphic creature taken out of a nightmare. Jamie shuddered at the idea and looked at Sean in amazement.

Sean "Isn't that amazing? The villagers told me about this plant. It is also called a good man because it obviously looks like a human and in the past it was used as an amulet to protect against disease and death. It tastes like mountain tea, you will like it. "

Sean took out of his pocket the small African knife he had bought from their last trip and with one movement removed the green part of the plant, separating it from its root. He washed the root in the sea, removing all the bumps, soil and hairs on it. He returned to the fire and cut Mandragora into small pieces in the kettle which was boiling. Jamie watched his movements, slightly dizzy from the wine she was drinking.

Jamie "You look like a witch on top of your cauldron making a potion." she told him laughing.

Sean "Strange that you say that. In ancient times it was believed that it has supernatural abilities and was associated with many superstitions! They also say that witches uprooted this plant at night like this one... with a full moon, because the cry of the plant that was heard when you uprooted it from the ground drove everyone crazy. "Only witches with their rituals could pick up Mandragora."

Jamie "Wow, I'm impressed! Where did you learn all this? You have enchanted me my love... I am literally hanging from your lips! Tell me more stories about Mandrake. "

Sean "I expected you to like it! They also believed that there was a man named Mandragoras and he reincarnated in this anthropomorphic figurehead to take revenge on the villagers who hanged him."

Jamie " Hang him, why? How did he get revenge? "

Sean "It's ready! Time to serve you my queen. "

Jamie "Won't you drink with me?"

Sean "No, my stomach hurts and I'm afraid it will get worse. Maybe I will drink some later."

Sean poured some of the broth to Jamie's glass and laid there hugged, gazing at the stars together. He stroked her hair and told her urban legends about Mandrake and when the broth in her glass ran out, he refilled it. Jamie listened to the stories with great interest and, finishing her third glass of Mandragora broth, remembered the question she had previously asked Sean.

Jamie "You didn't tell me baby, how would he take revenge on the villagers as a plant? You said he was reincarnated for that reason. I don't understand."

Sean poured the remaining liquid into the glass and squeezed her back into his arms again. Jamie felt cold and so he covered her with the knitted blanket they had next to the fire. Her hands began to tremble and her pupils were completely dilated. The look with which she was now looking at her lover was frightening.

Jamie "Tell me about Mandragora, my love"

Her body began to make jerky movements and Sean brought her closer to him holding her, one would say, with all his might! Tears ran down his face and dripped onto Jamie's head, which was no longer talking and seemed to have calmed down. Sean leaned over her and kissed her broth-flavored lips.

Sean "Mandragora Autumnalis!" he said, bursting into tears so loudly that he frightened the birds sleeping in the trees, high on the hill. Sean then continued his story. "The ancient Greeks and the Romans, used it as a hypnotic and sedative. Those in pain took a small amount of Mandragora to stop their pain and others used it to make erotic filters! The Greeks call it ' the apple of love ' and it is said that the witch Circe had given it to Odysseus' men to seduce them. " At this point Sean could not find the strength to continue and looked into Jamie's eyes.

Jamie "A little more my love, just a little bit more" she managed to whisper to him the words that barely came out of her mouth.

Sean "In the Middle Ages, however, it was used as a sedative for the dying... but even as the medicine that eventually took their lives... It is an opiate plant and its consumption in large quantities..." Sean's choking cry did not let him continue and broke out like a small child. The lifeless body of his beloved laid in his arms. Her face seemed to smile at him. Her eyes, fixed on the sky, remained wide open, looking at the stars one last time. Sean kept kissing his girl begging her to talk to him. His pain was unbearable but even more unbearable would be to live after what he did. But how could he do it, he thought! Several hours passed with Sean hugging her in front of the fire, which was now in danger of extinguishing. With the little courage he managed to find, he got up, gently resting Jamie's head on the knitted blanket that covered her and disappeared into the woods. After a few minutes he appeared again, only this time dragging something bulky behind him. Sean got back to where Jamie was and the flickering flame lit up the heavy object he was dragging with him. It was a raft.

You could also say it a boat but it looked more like a raft and that was the purpose. The raft was made of various dry logs, firmly joined next to each other and tied with string. On the raft he had placed several branches with leaves that had been dried by the sun. This raft was the reason that made Sean get up earlier than Jamie every day and go to the small grove behind their beach. The mystery was solved. Sean grabbed his wife's dead body, which was still warm, and put his head on her chest in one last attempt to hear her heart. After making sure that what he had done had no return, he lifted her in his arms and placed her on the raft. Sean fell over her and kissed her one last time. He had only one hour until dawn and the darkness, which tonight was his accomplice in the crime, disappeared for good. He got up and covered the rest of her body with twigs and dry leaves, poured some of the wine on the raft as a tribute to his dead wife and drank the rest. Then he caught a wood that was burning silently in the weak fire next to him and set the raft on fire. With quick movements he dragged it to the sea and began to swim in front of it, pulling it at the same time with all his strength, trying to move it away from the land as much as possible. The fire in the raft had intensified and was now enveloping the lifeless body of Jamie who was still wearing her wooden handmade wedding ring.

He then realized he had to leave her and go back to the beach but he just could not. He struggled with the water and tried to look at her a little more before she disappeared from his eyes once and for all! When the fire covered the whole raft burning everything on it and also the raft itself, Sean started swimming towards the shore. When he reached the beach, wet and terribly distressed, he looked up at the sky, looking for his God. The evil moon was there looking at him!

Sick Mind

Two months later he returned to their home in New York and a letter was waiting for him in their inbox. It was from her!

The months passed and New York was well into the heart of winter. Christmas was approaching and this was Jamie's favorite holiday! So he decided to decorate their house exactly as she would. Sean took down all the Christmas decorations from the attic and started decorating the house. He passed garlands on every column, placed the reindeers in their places, took out the lights and decorated their small balcony and dressed the chairs with festive covers. It was the tree's turn and he suddenly realized he could not stand decorate it all by himself. Jamie should have been there with him; he thought and sank in deep sadness. All the ornaments that she and he had chosen and bought together were there and they looked at him confused and angry. And there were many! He poured some of the whiskey into his glass and continued to unwrap them carefully, removing them from their transparent packaging and placing them one by one on the branches of the Christmas tree. Everything was perfect! Just as Jamie would have liked. But everything was so insignificant without her there. So colorless and so pointless. At that moment he remembered her letter. He had said that he would open it the moment he missed her the most! When his pain would be unbearable. Christmas day was definitely that day. So on Christmas night, he lit the fireplace to break the cold a bit, put the first drink he found in front of him and took Jamie's letter out of his nightstand drawer. He opened it and to his surprise there was no letter in the envelope. But there was a usb stick and that meant she had sent him an audio message or even better a video of her, he thought. His heart rate increased rapidly at the idea that he would see her again and his body went numb. He grabbed his laptop and sat on the couch in front of the Christmas tree. He took a deep breath and put the usb stick in one of the ports. He then opened the contents of the folder and click play in the only file it contained.

Her face was there! Her eyes were looking at him again! And the smile... oh that smile! Sean could not hold back his tears and he pressed the play button. The video showed Jamie a few months ago sitting in the same seat on the couch where her husband was now sitting. She was wearing a torn blouse with her favorite rock band which Sean used to tell her to throw away because it had become a rag and her short white jeans. Her hair was thrown over her shoulders and her hands were moving nervously in space. At the sound of her voice, Sean bent and Axel, with the little strength he had left, crawled to his feet, begging him to lift him into his arms. Sean took him in his arms and let him lie on him. Axl's old eyes were now looking at the screen and seemed to understand the sound and image they were looking at and listening. It was his best friend, Jamie. The video started and Jamie's voice flooded the living room.

Jamie "Hello pretty faces, how are you doing my love? I'll miss you both so very much! And if you are watching this video, you probably miss me too. Axl, my beautiful creature, how are you? My God, how much I miss you while I think about it. Sean, my love! Will you ever forgive me? Will you love me the same now that I am gone or did I make you hate me? You are the best thing that has happened to me Sean, you and this creature next to you. You are the best man I could have and I loathe myself for putting you in this situation. But we both know that it was the right thing to do. It may not have been fair to you but you know that I will be forever grateful to you baby. " at this point Jamie cried and trying to pull herself together she continued...

"Glioblastoma, what a stupid word! Just when I thought that the strongest asset on me was the brain, God comes and laughs at me! Oh! You think so Jamie?!!! Now I will show you! Cancer in the brain! " Her face had now changed, the tears stopped and the smile took its place again, on her beautiful face. " I'm sorry I have asked you of such a thing! Thank you for understanding my pain. You've always understood Sean. You were always by my side, more than I was to you, I would say. I love you for that! We would both have had very bad time Sean. I would have suffered but so would you, by my side. Things would have gotten much worse than a simple dizziness and a little vomiting. You know it yourself! "

Sean wiped his tears with the sleeve of his shirt and kissed Axl, who was making sad noises moving his head on each sound, unable to understand what had happened to his boss. Or was he crying because in his heart, he knew? Jamie's video continued for quite some time until it came to an end.

"My sweet babies, I get very angry that I won't be there with you. But I promise you that the three of us will meet again! In the next life! Our fate is woven with the same thread, continuously and in every life, we just have to wait for it to reunite us together! I want you to take care of each other and do things that will bring a smile back to your faces. I want you, Sean, to find a good girl, not as good as me or as cool as I am...but a little less and love again! " She said laughingly. " Of course I do not want you to love her as much as you loved me, but you understood what I am trying to say here... " she said laughing out loud, giving Sean his smile for a moment! "I want you to think of me and feel good, to love me and let me go and not think of the bad things Sean. I want you to try to forget the bad. I want you to promise me! This may seem difficult and impossible now, but together we can do it. Just because I'm not by your side does not mean I'll not see you, talk to you, or protect you. I will always be there Sean. In your heart and in your mind. I just want you to laugh when you think of me! What do you think? Can you do this for me? I love you Sean! I will always love you! I will look forward to the next life when we will meet again baby! Kisses to both of you! I love you! I love you very much! But you Sean, you my love, make my love seem so little in front of yours. You Sean really love me and with all your might. Mankind is terrified at the thought that there is such love, my baby. Never forget that! " The video ended, leaving behind sounds of Jamie's kisses to Sean and Axl, leaving them motionless, numb on the couch. Overwhelmed by the loss! At that moment, Sean decided it. He would return to their beach. He would return to her, to Petali and to the sea that took her away. It was the only thing on his mind that seemed logical. He would spend Christmas there and afterwards leave back for Greece for good. Suddenly, inside him, something calmed down and under the light of the flickering flame, he fell asleep on the couch.

Urban Myths

Thirty-six years later...

Elena "Well, it's really amazing!"

Thanos "I told you, you will love it! Wait until you dive, to see the crystal clear waters!"

Elena "I don't want to wait at all! I'm going in guys!!! " She said running towards the sea, throwing at the same time her clothes in the sand.

Irina "Let's set up the tents there, under the big rock. The sun will burn us here. "

Nicholas " We will have a problem under the rock! Mice will come to our food and at night you will hear sounds like pebbles falling on your tent."

Irina "Okay, I prefer the pebbles to the sun right on my freshly awaken eyes!"

Nikolas "They are not pebbles. Scorpios are falling. " he said smiling at her.

Irina "My God, you have brought me into the jungle! Ok and where are the toilets? "

Thanos and Nikolas burst out laughing.

Irina "Guys? Toilet, I say, where is it?? "

The boys laughed even louder and continued to set up their tents.

Elena "Well the water is unbelievable! Crystal clear and cold, I will never get bored of this place. When you leave, just leave me here! "

Irina "Did you know that there is no toilet?"

Elena "In fact, princess, we brought you for camping, I thought the absence of a toilet is self-evident!"

Nikolas "Elena, we can leave you doll, but will not last a month!"

Elena "I would endure much more than you my dear..."

Thanos " Yeah! You and John, the ghost of the beach."

Irina "Cut the crap or I'm out of here."

Nikolas " Dude, leave the horror stories for the night, around the fire! Muhahaha! " both boys laughed again. Nicholas pulled Irina into his arms and kissed her on the cheek.

Nikolas "Don't worry, dummass. You need to relax a bit, how will you enjoy the campsite if you won't let go? And what are you worried about? I am here." he told her and kissed her on the mouth this time.

The tents were ready and above them they had spread a military canopy, supported by five sticks. They had supplies for at least 20 days, maybe even more. The landscape was beautiful, so wild and mysterious that it attracted you to explore it. The flora had flooded the two hills that protected the small beach and scattered purple flowers decorated the hills. The tavern that existed above the forest was now deserted and seemed abandoned. There was only one blue boat outside in the yard, which was in good condition and waiting for someone to take it to the salty sea. The voices and laughter of the young campers, who were now swimming in the clear blue waters of the Aegean, echoed in the hills of Petali. Dusk came to their beach, turning the sky orange-red and the four friends came out of the water, in search of wood for their fire. Later, a stranger appeared in front of them as they placed the wood to light the fire. A boat was being dragged behind him.

Thanos "Good evening!"

The stranger was looking at them with his old and sunburnt face and did not bother to answer them. He lowered his hat to the ladies of the company, declaring his respect and continued to the sea, dragging the small blue boat together.

Nikolas "I hope we did not disturb you. We only want to enjoy your beach and the sea. We will not leave garbage when we leave, nor do we want riots." He said in an apologetic and respectful way.

The old man stopped at the sound of Nicolas words but did not turn to look at him a bit and when he finished his sentence he continued on his way again. Again he said nothing. He lifted the dark linen trousers he was wearing from his legs, threw his shoes into the boat which he then put in the water. Then he hopped in and within just a few minutes disappeared on the horizon. The others who were watching him did not say anything until he disappeared from their sight. The night had fallen and the fire was burning in front of them...

Irina "What was that now?"

Elena "It seemed to me that he wanted his peace and we ruined it for him."

Nicholas "But not to speak at all? How rude! It's our fault we said we would be gentlemen! Grab me a beer, Thanos. "

Thanos "He might not be able to talk you guys, relax. And why the long faces? He is an old man, what are you afraid of?!"

Elena "The question is what is he up to in the middle of the night in the dark sea?!"

Thanos "This does not surprise me. My father is also a fisherman and he goes out in the open many times in the early hours , hours before the sun rises."

Nicholas "However, I did not see a fishing rod; not even a line, my friend!"

Elena " Enough talking about the weirdo, guys, come on! Now…Tell me! "

Thanos "What?"

Elena "The stories with the ghosts you were talking about earlier. We are listening!!! "

Time passed and the young people seemed to enjoy their company. One story followed another and the alcohol in their blood made them even more exciting, even more frightening to their ears. Thanos, the eldest of the group, was a local and lived two villages away. He knew dozens of such mystery stories that he had heard since he was a small child. The other three in the group were children of the city but had known each other for years now. The four were students at the same university in Athens and were studying Medicine. This year was the last they all spent together because Elena would get her degree, Nikolas would go to his mother in Sweden, Thanos intended to stay in the place where he grew up in a hospital and Irina wanted at least two more years to graduate, maybe even more. They would spend this summer together, before they scatter all of them in different places. The bell of the small church on the hill rang twelve and took their breath away! They looked at each other and then looked up at the church looking for the man who rang the bell at this hour. There was no one in the church, which makes sense considering how late it was. But someone rang the bell and that was a fact!

Elena "Why are you rolling your eyes baby? Have you not heard of technology? The bell is probably connected to a timer and it rings every twelve hours. The scary thing is that you will become doctors now, seriously?! "

Thanos "Actually, there is no timer Elena. I know this church. I knew Father Athanasios who operated it until a few years ago, before he died, and he always rang it in the morning." His gaze was now fierce as he stared at the fire and looked a bit insane! The words coming out of his mouth sounded heavy and mysterious and the bell rang again! Everyone's eyes turned to the church bell tower but in the darkness no human figure stood out.

Irina "Do you want to tell me that in the middle of nowhere, in a deserted church in the dark, there is someone crazy up there who is ringing the bell and watching us?" Irina sounded more confused than the others who also found it difficult to give a logical answer.

Thanos "No, I'm not saying that. I think I know who he is. Father Athanasios. "

Nicholas "Didn't you asshole say that he died? Are you fucking with us? "

Thanos "Yes, he is dead. But his spirit has never left the church he had built himself. The villagers swear that they see him from time to time, or rather say, they hear him from time to time in the church! They also say that his spirit did not leave this beach to protect it from any evil. "

Nicholas, Irina and Elena burst out laughing loudly and immediately afterwards began to imitate Father

Athanasios making ridiculous representations of his spirit flying over the beach where they were. But Thanos did not laugh. His gaze consistently serious and pensive and he did not laugh at the nonsense of the others even for a moment.

Thanos "If the bell rings twice, there is no reason to worry."

The laughter stopped abruptly and everyone listened to their friend again carefully.

Thanos "If, however, the bell rings three times, then we have many reasons to worry and I am not laughing. This is not a joke!" Their friend now looked unusually serious and worried!

Elena "What do you mean?"

Thanos "When the bell rings three times the spirit of Father Athanasios means that he has found something really evil on the beach and will attack it to protect the village."

Nicholas "Dude, if you're kidding, just quit it now. What evil? To protect them from what? Come on, just tell us you are joking and get it over with! The girls have been scared enough, don't you think? . "

Thanos "I mean an evil person. Some stranger who comes here, like us, for example. Actually like you, because technically I am a local. Two years ago the body of a tourist was found on this beach and no one knows how he died. Rumor has it that he was coming from the capital every summer and approached underage girls and dragged them to this beach at night and then raped them. The cause of his death even in public documents that I personally went and searched, out of pure curiosity, does not exist. The residents are convinced that he... did it... "the bell rang for the third time and everyone started screaming! They got up from their seats panicked when they noticed that the fourth of the group was laughing!

Thanos " Gotcha!!! But how gullible are you really? Ouuuuuuuu!" he told them laughing while they were sitting around the fire again.

Thanos "You should have seen your stupid faces!"

Irina "My boy you are an idiot, that's why you will never find a girl!" she said visibly annoyed.

Elena "Nice! I liked it. Do you know other stories? I'm a fool for those urban legends. Then I will tell you some myself. "

Nikolas "Better leave it Thanos, save it for tomorrow. Can't you see here? " he said pointing to Irina who had not yet calmed down from Thanos' story.

Thanos "Well, I have one last for today. The best for the end! Jokes aside, this one is true! I won't say this just to scare you. I've been listening to this story from a young age from the elders of this island, even from my grandfather, that remembers it vividly. It took place thirty-six years ago, on this very beach... The month was August like now... and a young couple came to Petali to camp. The two lovers were in their thirties and had come from a foreign land. Some say they were Germans, others say Italians and others Americans. It does not matter. This couple cared and loved each other very much. The girl loved him like crazy and the man adored her. That's the reason no one understands why he did it! "

Irina "Did what? What did he do?"

Thanos "The night was the twenty-eighth of August and the moon was full and red. The only campers were these two alone. No other people around and for that there were never any witnesses. My grandfather tells me that John, which was the name of the girl's husband and whose name no one remembers…. as I was saying, John, killed his beloved that August night and threw her into the sea! Since then, the girl appears every night on the beach and cries mourning her lost love that from what it seemed in the end wasn't that big! Others say that he did not love her and just killed her, others that he did it for the life insurance she had, for the money while other prejudicial superstitions and gossips of a group of people who believe in the magical abilities of the moon, say that their love was real and that the red moon drove him crazy! That it got jealous seeing them every night making love and drove John madly jealous who in the end blindly killed her …! "

When the story of Thanos ended, they realized that they were not alone! The stranger they had seen earlier in the afternoon was coming out of the sea in front of them, pulling his wooden boat behind him. Thanos then continued…

Thanos "John's pain was unbearable when he realized what he had done to his beloved and since then he goes back on the beach every single night till this very day and fights with the moon, looking at the Black Sea, waiting..."

Elena "What was he waiting for every night?

Stranger man "Waiting to see her! He was looking at the sea and waiting for her to appear and talk to him."

Suddenly everyone stopped talking and looked at the stranger next to them, who magically appeared out of nowhere, in the night and listened to their conversation.

Elena "Do you know this story too? Did you know John or his wife? Are you from here? "

Stranger Man "His name is Sean. And hers, Jamie! And he loved her. " he growled and picked up his boat again to leave. Nicholas turned on the flashlight he had in his pocket and shed light on the name on the boat, which he just remembered he had seen earlier that day. JAMIE!

Living Nightmare

New York, 24.07.2020

"JAMIE, JAMIE, JAMIE girl!!! "Wake up at last, did you fall asleep Jamie girl?" a tall gentleman, elegantly dressed and with feminine features, appeared at the reception. Rochel, Jamie's French colleague, was around forty-five with slightly gray hair and seemed very interesting as a person, smartly dressed and with good posture like coming out of a fashion magazine. Unable to wake her up, he started shouting at her, hoping that this way he would succeed. "JAMIIIIIE, JAMIIIIIIIIIIE" He screamed at his sleeping colleague and after grabbed his throat which seemed to be irritated by the voices!

Jamie jumped in the air and rolled her eyes. The chair slid backwards, creaking, making them both startle. Jamie had finally woken up!!!

Rochel "My sweet girl, did you really manage to sleep here?!"

Jamie "What did I do? I was sleeping?"

Rochel "And in fact quite heavy! I tried for at least ten minutes but who knows what you were seeing and did not want to wake up? Tell me...!" he told her in a playful mood, something Jamie did not seem to have at all.

Jamie "What time is it, Rochel?"

Rochel "Eleven and a half... I know... sorry I was late, Abed is to blame, he delayed me! But seriously look it up, it's not normal. Can you imagine someone coming inside taking the money from the cash register? Mrs. Orwell would have a stroke! " he was talking to her while she was combing her hair that were flying here and there. Jamie burst out laughing while tears flowed from her eyes.

Rochel "Are you crying? My God, baby what happened? What did I say, the idiot? "

Jamie was laughing now and her face seemed to calm down as she recovered from her nightmares.

Jamie "I was having crazy dreams and they were so alive! I shudder just thinking about it, they felt so alive Rochel! " Rochel had grabbed the second chair at the front desk and when he got comfortable he nod at Jamie to continue!

Jamie "I saw my parents and grandparents, people I met ten years ago, I saw representations of my life with Sean... and the strange thing is that most of these were real! I mean, they have happened, but it was like experiencing them for the first time! I honestly have never experienced anything like it before. It's scary if you think about it! My mind played so many scripts, a proper movie and many of them I don't remember now if you ask me. But I remember myself as a child. I was a very anxious child growing up but in my dream I saw me doing crazy things, which never really happened but the conditions were actually the same. The places, however, along with the people who were there, were all true. You would say the script was different... oh, all this truly upset me, and what time is it? "

Rochel "Leave the time be... tell me now, did you have sex with anyone or did you sleep for so many hours for nothing?" he said laughing.

Jamie "Sex eh? Hmmm ... I do not remember! I think so." then Jamie's face darkened again and she stood there cold as ice staring at Rochel.

Rochel "Jamie? What is it?"

Jamie "I remembered the end! Sean killed me, I was sick and he killed me to save me from the pain."

Rochel "Even in your nightmares this man is a saint!!! Unbelievable! How bored I am of your sickening love. "

Jamie "Axel keeps me awake lately and I don't sleep well. Some female dog is probably the problem... and the poor thing he does everything to get himself out of the house! He has been on a hunger strike for three days now. My lover boy! " she said with a smile.

Rochel "Ah bring him some day over here, how old is he now?"

Jamie "He's three years old... Are you crazy? And what will I say? Hello, today I have brought my dog to keep me company because I'm bored? "

Rochel "No. Tell them I brought him as a guard because I am sleeping upright! " he said and laughed out loud.

Jamie "Wow, the time has passed, Axl will be hungry and Sean will be looking for me. Need to go."

Rochel "My greetings to your handsome husband..."

Jamie "Watch your saliva... is running! Good night sweetie! "

Rochel "Au revoir Jamie!"

Jamie left the Emerald Street Hotel, got on her electric skate and headed home. The wind was beating on her face, dispelling any sign of dizziness caused by the intense heat of July. The drive home was very interesting and particularly enjoyable as she passed through the lush Central Park. Of course it was evening at that time and you could not see the ducks on the lake or the small picturesque restaurants that were housed there. One might also say that it was actually quite a dangerous route at this time. You only saw dark figures walking and the beautiful elegant lights in each alley of the park were not enough to fully illuminate the environment, which now made Jamie regret that she chose this path to get home! She herself was not an easily feared girl, but she thought she was still affected by those nightmares earlier. Some images had not completely left her mind, no matter how hard she tried and some of the stories she saw unfolding in her sleep were unfortunately true! The truth is that most of all, she tried to get these ones out of her mind. With that in mind, Jamie had already reached the front door of her house. She looked up at the second-floor window where the living room was. Sean had returned from work.

"Love" Potion

New York, 24.12.2020

The second-floor window was festively decorated with green and red garlands and a three-dimensional sticker of a reindeer trying to get inside the house was stuck on it. Some snowflakes were sitting on the terrace of the window looking at the Christmas tree, which illuminated the whole living room with its lights. The other lights were off and a woman with a bloated belly seemed to be sleeping on the white sofa in front of the fireplace. The door of the house opened and at the sound of the keys touching the table, the woman woke up and opened her eyes.

Jamie "Baby? Is that you Sean?"

Jamie was now trying to get up from the couch that was lying so comfortably but her six-month-old belly was making her every move difficult.

Jamie "Baby are you back? I fell asleep on the couch again. Where are you?"

Jamie had now gotten up from the couch and was walking down the hallway leading to the door of their house. Sean did not seem to have heard her and probably that is why he did not answer her, she thought. Arriving at the corridor, she noticed that Sean was indeed there and was putting a tiny bottle in his jacket when he noticed her presence. Jamie could not see exactly the small object that Sean was trying to keep secret and thought it might be her gift that he had not yet managed to wrap.

Sean "Hey, what are you doing awake at this hour? I told you I would be late today. What is our little one doing? " he told her and stroked her belly.

Jamie "Don't worry, I was asleep, your keys woke me up. I fell asleep on the couch again. I am befuddled by the fire from the fireplace and the lights in the Christmas tree and I sleep well here. Why were you late today?"

Sean "We had a lot of work, on days like this we all work overtime. At least they will pay me more! Come on, since you're awake let's go open the presents, Christmas Eve today. "

Jamie "Yeah, that's what I'm saying, Christmas Eve and you've been working. Anyway, let's go open them. Axl, come on my boy " The little brown dog ran happily behind her wagging his tail.

Sean "Here's your gift, I hope you like it!"

Jamie took the red envelope in her hands and knew that this was not the only gift he would give her as the little bottle in Sean's pocket would probably have to wait. She opened the file excitedly and saw the content she was now holding in her hands.

Jamie "Tickets to Greece? Wow baby thank you! Why are there no dates? "

Sean "I thought of buying them open, without setting a date. So we could leave whenever you want, or whenever we can anyway. You do not look very excited Jamie. Didn't you like my idea? "

Jamie "Yes, of course I liked it. I just felt a little weird. I remembered the nightmare I had. It still haunts me for some reason and doesn't go away. Of course I liked your gift, come here! "

Sean "Which nightmare? That day you slept at work you mean? You never told me about that dream. Maybe if you tell me and get it out of your system, it will stop torturing you! Don't forget that they are just dreams...! "

Jamie leaned over to kiss him and then they opened the rest of the presents. They later saw a black-and-white movie playing that was taking too long to finish and all three of them fell asleep on the couch. Jamie woke up from another nightmare and noticed that the fire in the fireplace was out. Axl was sleeping on her feet and so she got up slowly and carefully so as not to wake him. Sean seemed to be sleeping soundly and covered him with the blanket she had on her. Jamie walked to the toilet and thought that she would sleep half an hour a day and be visiting the toilet the rest of the remaining time. Only three months were left for her to give birth, Sean probably did not think of that when he booked the tickets.

How would they go abroad? Where would they be leaving the baby? Newborns are not allowed to fly. Or is it allowed? And the baby's ticket where was it? She closed the toilet door behind her and started walking towards the living room when she stopped. An inexplicable desire to search Sean's coat for her second gift overwhelmed her and despite her efforts not to do so, her curiosity won out! Jamie walked down the aisle, where their coats were hanging and quietly grabbed Sean's jacket. She put her hand in his front pocket and she suddenly felt it. It was indeed a glass bottle, probably some expensive perfume! She reverently took the unknown object in her hands and processed it.

The bottle was quite small and strangely heavy for its size. It was all glass and the liquid it contained was intensely dark, like black or burgundy, but with the lights off she could not be sure. The lid was tightly closed with sealing wax, which is very strange for perfume but maybe it was handmade and thus ensured the quality of the perfume. *Who knows*! She thought and lifted the bottle in the air so that she could see its inscription. The inscription was written in calligraphic characters and this made it difficult for Jamie to read. She was ready to give up, so as not to spoil the surprise when the Latin writing she was looking at made sense. Her gaze froze and her heart stopped when the letters on the bottle cleared. '*Mandragora Autumnalis*' The small bottle fell from her hands and hit the thick red carpet she was walking on. The lights in the hallway came on and Jamie frightened looked up at the man staring at her. Sean was standing at the end of the aisle. He looked insanely angry...

Dark Affairs

Eight months later…

New York, 14.09.21

The dishes in the kitchen sink had been stacked and the shutters were hermetically sealed. One could say, seeing them, that there has been a long time since someone opened them and cleaned them as they were particularly dusty. The TV was mute, playing cartoons in the children's program. The sofa had three different sheets on it and some T-shirts and socks were thrown here and there on the floor. A man was lying face down on the couch and his hand was holding a bottle of whiskey, which was standing on the dirty floor. The sound of the cell phone was suddenly heard and although it was very loud, it took a long time for the sleeping man to realize it was ringing! In an attempt to grab the phone, he threw it from the small coffee table and knocked it on the floor. To his great annoyance, the phone kept ringing and so he had to gather all his strength to manage and pick it up.

Sean "Yes."

Inspector Sally "Good morning Mr. Bailey! I hope I'm not interrupting."

Sean "Who is it? Of course you're interrupting... my sleep, sir! That's unacceptable, calling people in the middle of the night! "

Inspector Sally "Mr. Bailey, I am Inspector Sally, I have taken over your wife's case and we were waiting for you to return from your vacation. I have some more questions, you see."

Sean "And you could not wait Inspector Sally for the sun to shine and then call me? I did not expect midnight calls from the police, the truth is."

Sally "Mr. Bailey, it is ten o'clock. In the morning! I just wanted to confirm that you are at home before I visit! I will be there in half an hour. I would advise you to throw some cold water on your face and wake up. We have a lot to talk about!"

Sean looked at the wall clock, which showed ten past five, and hurriedly got up from the couch, accidentally kicking the whiskey bottle that got spilled on the wooden floor.

The suitcases from his recent trip abroad were still in the hall and he had not managed to open them yet. The house was chaotic and this image was completed by the dozens of pizza boxes that were thrown carelessly around. Sean hurried to pick them up as time passed quickly and the inspector would come in any minute now. He did not want him to see the house in this mess, so he began to gather the clothes he had thrown everywhere, changing the ones he was already wearing when he realized that they smelled really bad. He was pouring water on his face when he heard the doorbell ring. The inspector had come. He wiped his face quickly and with nervous movements straightened his hair a bit. On the way to the front door, he remembered the bottle of whiskey he had thrown on the floor earlier, but thought he no longer had time to pick it up, so he opened the door.

Sean "Good morning Inspector! Huh, look at this, exactly half an hour, as you said...! You weren't joking with the time; please come in."

Inspector Sally "My wife claims that my sense of humor is quite poor and I believe her. " He said entering the house, while exploring the area with his piercing eyes. "I married a smart woman, I would like to believe, so I have no reason to joke around, Mr. Bailey! " he said, taking off the hat he was wearing, placing it on the furniture next to him. "Well? Where do we sit? "

Sean "Over here, please ..." he said, pointing to the living room because the kitchen was in a bigger mess! "I thought Sally was a female name, so that's how you were baptized?" he said in a calming tone trying to lighten the mood.

Inspector Sally "Sally is my last name, Mr. Bailey. But as far as I know it is a neutral name for girls and boys. Shall we begin now? " he said and sat down on the white couch Sean had pointed out to him. "Is that whiskey I smell?" he said, smelling the air around him, looking at Sean.

Sean "Yes, I accidentally knock down my glass yesterday and the smell is not gone yet. It has watered the wood for good. " he said with a nervousness in his gaze.

Inspector Sally "I did not come here to criticize you for your drinking, whether you use a glass or not, Mr. Bailey." he said, taking out the bottle of whiskey under the couch, placing it on the table. "As an adult you can do whatever you want. But it would be nice if you did not lie to me unnecessarily. You are not helping me like that, nor your own self! "

Sean "Yes, of course. I didn't have much time to tidy up the place so I forgot some things. I was embarrassed to admit that I slept with the bottle in my hands. Tell me inspector, how can I help you in your research? I thought the case was closed and your visit here shook me the truth is. Did you say that you have new information? "

Inspector Sally "Everything on time, Mr. Bailey. First I would like to ask you some general questions, if you'll allow me." he said and opened a small notebook he took out of his jacket pocket.

Sean "Please, I'm at your disposal, although I honestly don't understand."

Inspector Sally "Do not worry, Mr. Bailey, first things first! Now tell me, when did you plan your trip to Greece? "

Sean "I don't remember exactly, it was just before Christmas, it was my gift to Jamie."

Inspector Sally "And why did you choose to leave the dates open?"

Sean "We didn't know when we would be able to leave and if we even could after the birth..." at that point he hesitated a little and his face darkened at the thought of his unborn child... and continued... "As I said, we did not know when we would finally be able to travel. »

Inspector Sally "Is there any reason that the tickets were two Mr. Bailey while you would be three? I mean you were expecting a child... »

Sean "I understand what you mean. No, there was no reason, I probably did not think it right. Maybe I guessed it would not be able to travel being a newborn and so I booked us two. I was very excited when I booked the tickets, I was not thinking clearly. I don't know what else to say. "

Inspector Sally "Perhaps, yes," said Sally, looking at him now with his piercing black eyes. "Some would say you were planning to do this trip on your own. Without your wife or the baby. As it happened as a matter of fact! What do you have to say on this?"

Sean "What are you saying? Who is accusing me of all this? They do not respect my mourning and they gossip around; are these your new facts Mr. Sally; Is that why you are bothering me today? "

Inspector Sally "I am sorry if I bothered you, in your mourning... I also apologize if I offended you. Tell me, Mr. Bailey, how many days have passed since you returned from your voyage to the Mediterranean? " He said, noting something in his small book.

Sean "It's been about a week, why do you ask?" he said, visibly agitated by the discussion.

Inspector Sally "I noticed the suitcases in the hallway as I entered. Are you planning to go anywhere else?

Sean "No, these are the suitcases I had with me on the trip, I had no time to unpack."

Inspector Sally "Mr. Bailey, you have a week back and your suitcases are untouched. You claim that you did not have time and from what I see the house is a big mess, is everything ok with you? Is there anything you do not tell me? "

Sean "Mr. Inspector, as you said at the beginning of our discussion, I am an adult and I have the right to unpack my suitcases whenever I want. And now if you allow me I have somewhere to be and I would not want to run late. "

Inspector Sally "I just don't understand why you would do it," Sally said as he got up from the couch.

Sean froze and stared at him. His eyes looked frightened now and his lips were trying to articulate the next word.

Sean "What do you think I did, Inspector?"

Inspector Sally "I do not understand how you were able to make this trip, when your wife had just passed away. Where did you find the appetite and the courage? I don't understand that, Mr. Bailey." he said and put his little notebook back in his pocket.

Sean "I asked the inspector if I could leave before I did of course! I asked the person in charge of the case back then and he gave me the permission. Besides, I would not had left forever, at some point I would return. As you well can see … »

Inspector Sally "Alas, Mr. Bailey. But that was not my question… "he said and opened the door of the house to leave. "I would suggest you not to go on a trip this time, Mr. Bailey. I will be needing you for a little while more, I'm afraid. " he said and closed the door of his green car.

Sean was standing at the door of his house, watching Inspector Sally's green car disappear after the turn. Things were not as he expected, returning from his journey, he thought and a shiver went through his body. He hoped everything had been forgotten by then. The wooden door of the house closed behind him and he looked for the bottle of whiskey on the table. There were still two or three sips left inside.

The next morning found Sean sleeping on the sofa in his living room once again. The sound of the front doorbell woke him from the dream he was seeing and he turned his side in an attempt to continue his sleep. But whoever was behind the door seemed quite persistent and continued to ring the bell furiously, until in the end he succeeded! Sean, irritated, got up from the couch and walked lazily towards the entrance of his house. He opened the door and saw Inspector Sally in his characteristic hat, smiling at him.

Inspector Sally "Good morning, Mr. Bailey! I hope I did not wake you up. "

Sean "You basically did, inspector, you know you could pick up the phone before you decide to visit me."

Inspector Sally "Yes, yes, I agree. That's why I called you three times before I came over, Mr. Bailey. Obviously you sleep heavily and did not hear it. Now can I enter or do you prefer us to go to the police department to continue our conversation? " he said continuing to smile.

Sean "Come on in. I thought our conversation was over. After all, I have told you what I know, I do not understand why all these questions again. "

The two men had already moved inside the house and were now sitting at the kitchen table.

Inspector Sally "You're right, Mr. Bailey. On my previous visit I failed to inform you, you see, you were in a hurry to leave. Really, where did you go?"

Sean "I went to Boston to visit my mother. I would have missed the train, that's why I politely asked you to leave."

 Inspector Sally "Indeed. You did not exactly ask me that politely, but let it be. So back in our case. If you have to prove to me that you visited your mother, Mr. Bailey, will you be able to do so? "

Sean "But of course. Although I hope it will not be needed. It seems to me that you are treating me as if I am a guilty of something. I told your colleague Mr. Trigger everything I knew and we had a great cooperation. Should I start worrying? "

 Inspector Sally "You know better, Mr. Bailey, of which things you need to worry about. My dear colleague, Mr. Trigger, recently retired, I have no doubt that he did a good job, but still, he is old and may have inadvertently missed some important clues. The reason I am in this case is because Jamie's mother, a dear friend of mine, begged me. She is my childhood friend you see and I could not deny this to her. So in the beginning, while I wasn't waiting for something that was worth investigating, in a closed, as it seemed ,case, soon something changed my mind!

Sean got up nervously from the kitchen table that separated him from the inspector and looked really worried even though he made a great effort not to show it. The Inspector then continued.

Inspector Sally " I've asked you, Mr. Bailey, not to leave the country because I would need your help. Jamie's mother is convinced that you know a lot more than you say and she requested from us not to close the case."

Sean "We have a very good relationship with Lucy, I don't understand why she did not inform me of her intentions. What makes her think I'm lying? "

Inspector Sally "No one said Mr. Bailey that you lied! She just thinks you have information that you have not disclosed. She is a mother and often the mother's instinct comes out right! "

Sean "Something tells me she's not the only one who believes this ..."

Inspector Sally "Very well! When I took over the case of your dead wife, Mr. Bailey, I started my investigation from scratch. So when I came across the note that Jamie had left to you, I couldn't but start my research on the case right from the beginning."

Sean "What do you mean inspector?"

The inspector then removed a sheet of paper from the file on the table, which was enclosed in a slide. Held the paper with both hands and he read its contents.

"My dear Sean, I did not want to say goodbye to you like this and I ask you to forgive me for what will follow. I'm weak Sean and I cannot hide it anymore. I suffer and I make you suffer too my love and I do not want it. It is beyond my strength now and I can no longer fight the demons. I want you to take care of yourself and my beloved Axl and think of me sometime. Think of our good times and not the bad ones. Thank you for everything you have done for us and I hate myself for doing this to you, causing you so much pain. I hope one day you will forgive me and understand me.

Your wife

Jamie... '

The inspector folded the paper again and placed it in the slide and then in the gray envelope in front of him. He looked up at Sean, who was already sweating in the sound of the content of the letter and was now wiping his face with his sleeve.

Inspector Sally "Are you okay, Mr. Bailey? Can I bring you some water? You are pale. "

Sean "Sorry, Inspector, It's been a long time since I've last read it and the feelings overwhelmed me. I will be fine. But I don't understand what you want to say by reading it again. "

Inspector Sally "The letters, Mr. Bailey. The letters on the paper do not match the graphic character of your wife at all! You should have seen it, of course. It is so obvious! My good colleague Trigger failed to look at it properly and so when I got it in my hands I looked for other letters hand written by the deceased. I found out, as you can understand, that it would have been impossible for Jamie to have written this letter since she herself was left-handed and this letter was written by a right-hand person. Also the graphic character in the letter found, as I said, has nothing to do with the real one! "

Sean "What do you mean, Mr. Sally?"

Inspector Sally "The obvious Mr. Bailey. Your wife was killed! I have reopened the case of course and we are no longer talking about suicide. I will need a list of her acquaintances as well as those who according to you could harm her. Everything you know can be useful to us, even the slightest thing. Tell me, Mr. Bailey, did your wife have an extramarital affair?"

Sean "I would like to believe that no, inspector."

Inspector Sally " Yes, we all want to believe that, of course. Only the way she left, how to say it, was a bit romantic if you will allow me. That's why in the beginning it perfectly matched the scenario of the suicide. Mandrake solution... hm we are still trying to find the beginning of the skein with this poison. Sooner or later we will find the traces of the one who sold it to her. As long as we follow the facts... and Jamie's killer has left many of them unintentionally... "

Sean "Really? Is there evidence? Like what?" he said in an almost trembling voice and sat down in the chair in front of him.

Inspector Sally "Oh! My dear, but of course there is evidence. In murder cases, the killer rarely moves carefully in the scene, especially if something unforeseen happens and he is caught off-guard. Take for example also the famous quote 'the killer always returns to the crime scene' and believe me that is very true. Unless, of course, that so happens and the crime scene, is also his home! " he said jokingly and laughed.

Sean "What do you mean by this inspector? That I killed my wife; You do not need to hide behind jokes and cheap hints, whatever is that you have to tell me say it as a man inspector. I have nothing to hide. I loved Jamie." he said angrily and got up from his chair again irritated.

Inspector Sally "Mr. Bailey, I unintentionally made a bad joke. I did not want to upset you. But I'm not hiding from you the fact that you are one of our main suspects and if of course you want you can always talk to your lawyer first, although I do hope you will cooperate with us. After all, we want the same thing. You will not be able to be informed of any developments in the matter unless I deem it necessary. And now forgive me, Mr. Bailey, but I must leave. My wife has cooked stuffed vegetables and is my favorite meal! "

Sean "Yes, of course you can call me whenever you need. Inspector Sally?! May I ask you something? Are you sure it was not suicide?"

 Inspector Sally "More confident than the fact the earth is spinning, Mr. Bailey. Have a good afternoon!" he said putting on his hat and went down the stairs to the front door.

At the same time, Sean closed the door of his house and headed for the kitchen. He opened the cupboard with the glasses and took out two short ones, used for serving liqueurs. He grabbed the bottle of whiskey that was now plentiful in the house and poured its content until both glasses overflowed. He picked one up and said "Cheers Jamie, you did it again!" and with two sips drank both glasses. Then he poured some more whiskey into his glass and grabbed his cell phone. Dialed a number and waited... After several attempts the person on the other end of the line picked up the phone and a heavy female voice was heard.

Andria "We said you wouldn't call me again."

Sean "There is a problem."

Andria " Especially if there was a problem you should not have called me, Sean!"

Sean "I just wanted to know if any cop approached you latetly."

Andria "No. But if you keep calling me, it will not be long before they connect the dots. Look I did not want to do it but the money was a lot and the last thing I want is not to have time to enjoy the cash! Don't call me again, for your own sake... »

The line dropped and the charming woman sat in the antique armchair that was next to her. She lit her cigar and took a deep breath, exhaling the smoke slowly as if enjoying it. In her hands she wore various colorful bracelets and her fingers were all covered with gold and silver rings. Her face evoked mysticism and the turban she wore over her long golden hair complemented the image of mystery. There were infinitely small items and large old furniture in the space around her and the shop windows were full of perfumes in small and large bottles, each different from the other. The perfumes looked handmade and were very eye-catching. Every woman would go crazy in there. But the space was suffocatingly small and one would wonder how well all these objects could fit in there. Outside the small shop with the lights off, a sign hung. *"Andria's antiques"*. The charming lady got up from her velvety chair, walked to the glass entrance door and looked out on the street. Then she turned the label with the inscription 'open' that hung on the door, on the other side and continued to smoke her cigar.

Guilt

That night, as every night lately, Sean drowned his grief in another bottle of alcohol. The last couple of weeks, he drank all the time and every hour of the day and the next morning he would found himself unconscious on the living room couch or even at the kitchen table, but never in his own bed. Jamie's death tormented him and he had probably realized lately that he would never get rid of that burden. Day by day he was getting worse and had also stopped going to work until eventually he was fired. However, the money from Jamie's insurance was enough for him to spend the next few years without having to worry about his finances at all. The fear, on the other hand, that sooner or later he would be blamed, was constantly on his mind and this did not facilitate him to behave more logically but made him even more anxious in his behavior. The inspector had seen this, he thought himself! He was very close to unmask him. And with these thoughts he fell asleep exhausted from the alcohol in his blood. The dreams he was seeing, when falling unconscious from the drinking, felt much alive and so even asleep he could no longer escape his remorse. He watched Jamie wander around their house again, as if she had never left. He saw her crouching over his head and caressing him as she used to when she found him sleeping; and he heard her sing softly to him as she went up to their bedroom, enchanting him to follow her! Sean wanted to get up and hug her again but his body did not obey the commands of the mind! He felt that he was sleeping heavily and yet her presence was so intense in the space around him. Other times he thought he was opening his eyes from sleep and Jamie was standing there in front of him sad, constantly asking him why he did it. Why did he kill her?! At those times he was waking up suddenly drenched in sweat, running to the bathroom to pour water on his face. The sound of her voice constantly asking him 'why', did not leave his mind and almost drove him completely crazy! Who knows, he wondered, maybe this was his punishment. And he opened a new bottle seeking solace.

The days passed and soon December came again. The cold outside on the streets was harsh and white thick snow had now covered the streets of New York. The light from Sean's bedroom was on, the window was open and Sean stood there motionless and naked. The snowflakes that came inside, melted as they rested on the red carpet of the room. The nightmare he had just seen and ran to the window to be struck by the cold air and recover, seemed very real! Jamie had appeared in front of him again tonight, only this time she opened his mouth as he slept and watered him a little from the filter he had given her, on that fatal night. When Sean woke up from the nightmare, he would swear he heard a noise in the bedroom and ran into his blur to find the man who had invaded his house. When he arrived, however, he realized that his imagination was playing games, so he opened the window to be hit by the cold breeze. He had completely lost his peace of mind and felt extremely tired. His nightmares along with inspector Sally's continuous visits put so much pressure on him that they made him paranoid. The few times you found him sober and awake nowadays, was recollecting those beautiful days when he had Jamie by his side and immediately felt so bad that threw himself back into drinking again. He preferred it, from the pain he felt inside when he was sober. He no longer cared whether he would go to jail. And what would he not give to hold her in his arms again. Like that night, before she told him she wanted a divorce. Before she broke his heart into a thousand pieces. Before announcing that she would leave him once and for all. Before he takes her life! Before all that... when they were both happy!

The window sealed with a loud click and Sean sat on their bed for the first time in a long time. The room was as they had left it a year ago, nothing had changed. On the bedside table by Jamie there was a book and a cherry-scented oil, which she used to burn before going to bed. A blue silk ribbon hung from her lamp and there were pictures of her, Sean and Axl on the walls. Sean could not hold back the tears that were now running like a river over him. With the little strength his body had at that moment, he got up and opened the closet. There he saw his wife's colorful clothes and soon memories flooded his head. He touched the clothes, as if it was Jamie under the fabrics wearing them and he was in fact touching her and not the soulless cloth. He had missed her so much. How crazy was he to ever think he could live without her? But even if he could, regrets would certainly not let him escape so simply! He looked at the clothes in the closet for a while until he found what he was looking for! Her wedding dress was on a pink velvet hanger! He took it in his hands and pulled it out. He hugged it with all his might and cried like he had never cried in his life. He reverently placed Jamie's wedding dress on the bed and straightened the wrinkles with his hands. Then he lay down on the bed next to it and suddenly Jamie showed up next to him, wearing her wedding dress!

Jamie "What is it my love? Why are you so sad? Didn't you want that? " she spoke to him as if she were really by his side, with wet and melancholy eyes, with a sweetness in her voice and a warm smile that made his heart melt. Her big eyes were now looking at him waiting for an answer.

Sean "Jamie I am sorry... truly sorry, sorry, sorry, I did not want it, I do not know what got into me my love, I am sorry I don't want to live without you anymore." he collapsed on a sobbing heap, hugging the dress, feeling Jamie at his every touch.

Jamie "Don't apologize my darling, stay strong for us."

Sean "For you?"

Jamie "Yes... for me and your son..."

Now Jamie's face had changed dramatically and was replaced by a macabre creature that bore little resemblance to her. Sean jumped out of bed and hit his back in the closet behind him. The face he was looking at now had dark black eyes and its skin was burned and torn. Jamie's legs had been transformed into roots and the blue dress on the bed was soiled. Sean's heart was pounding like crazy and he was out of breath. This eerie thing he was looking at was not his Jamie! He quickly fell to his knees and began to scream in his paranoia. The creature in Jamie's position was smiling at him and blood was flowing from its mouth. It held out its hands to Sean and when Sean saw what it was holding he stopped shouting. He froze! In the hellish creature hands was a beautiful pink baby. The baby was alive and looking into the eyes of Sean who had now taken it in his arms. He smiled at the little angel he was holding and the little one smiled too! The disgusting dungy idol that has scared him before had been replaced again in the form of Jamie, who was now more beautiful than ever! She smiled at Sean and got out of bed to pick up the little baby.

Jamie "I will call him Mandrake..." she said as she took the little one from Sean's hands. "When he grows up I will tell him that he got his name from a poisonous plant... With that your father killed you, so I will tell him!" the ghost said to Sean and left beside him. Now she was standing in front of the window and after taking one last look at Sean, she dived into the gap in front of her. Sean screamed and ran to her but it was too late. Jamie was lost once and for all. He sat on the bed and looked at his hands. They were full of blood. The phone rang and Sean went down to the living room where he had it to pick it up, but by the time he got there it had stopped ringing. Sean realized he was not sleeping. He was awake. Everything that had just happened was not just a dream or a nightmare. He must have imagined them! There was no other explanation. He poured some whiskey in a mug he found in front of him when the phone rang again. Sean got scared at the sound and threw the mug with the drink on the floor. Jamie appeared in front of him and told him to pick up the phone and that she would clean the mess. Sean obeyed picked up the phone.

Sean "Yes."

Lucy "Son? How are you doing my child? It has been a long time since you've called us Sean. "

Sean "Lucy what are you doing? I'm fine, fine! I'm here with your daughter; she's cleaning up my mess. Clumsy me! How is Axl doing? We were thinking of spending the next few days in Poughkeepsie and take him home with us. We've missed him!"

Lucy "What are you saying? Who will come to get Axel? "

Sean "Me and Jamie you silly! One moment, let me give the phone to her..."Sean looked at Jamie in front of him and gave her the phone but she smiled and told him she had to get the baby dressed and get ready to leave.

Lucy "Are you there? What happened?"

Sean "Yes, Lucy, she can't talk to you right now, she's getting the little one ready for school. She will call you back ok? Many kisses to you and Axl, bye bye for now! "

The phone fell from Mrs. Lucy's trembling hands who, terrified by what she has heard, was trying to hold back her tears but in vain. She picked up the phone again from the floor and dialed a number.

Inspector Sally "Sally is speaking!"

Lucy "Martin I'm Lucy!"

Inspector Sally "Hey Lucy, what happened?"

Lucy "Martin, I just hung up with Sean. Something is wrong. I think Sean has lost it! "

Inspector Sally "What do you mean he lost it?"

Lucy "Yeah, I got him on the phone and he sounded so happy! I asked him what he was doing and he told me that he was there with Jamie and they were getting ready to take the little one to school. He wanted to give her to me on the phone to talk to her! Ah Martin, I will really go crazy. I do not know what is happening but I think he killed my little girl! You have to help me Martin, only you can help me! "

Inspector Sally "Come on Lucy, don't cry. The truth is that I would have called you myself today, we had some developments. But first I wanted to go there myself to investigate and I would have called you later. However, what you are telling me now is very strange. I have to go to Sean's house today and see him. If it is true that he went crazy then we may be lucky and he will tell us the truth."

Lucy "God bless you Martin. I will be waiting to hear from you!"

The Beginning of the End

Inspector Sally hung up the phone and got up from his office chair. He put on his hat, took his trench coat in his hands and got into his old green car. After half an hour he arrived in a neighborhood with many small shops, which were mostly owned by Chinese and Russian immigrants. He parked his car by the road and got out. Smells from a Chinese restaurant in the corner reached his nose and he thought he might sit down after and eat some soup. It would do good to his cold and it would be exactly what he needed this winter day. He walked for a minute along the sidewalk and when he reached his destination he stopped and looked at the sign. *'Andria's Antiques'*

Inspector Sally "Good evening! Is anybody here?" he said addressing the non-existent owner of the small shop. " Good Evening! Who is in charge here please? " he shouted again in the shop but no answer from anywhere! Inspector Sally walked around the antiquary and began exploring the antiques around. Several objects there made a great impression on him and he was now processing them in his hands. The owner seemed to be absent and all he could do was to wait for him to show up. His eyes now fell on the shop windows with the countless small vials with the strange names. He tried to open the glass that guarded them but in vain. The window was locked.

Andria "Hello, can I help you?"

The figure of a beautiful lady appeared behind him and frightened the inspector. This woman was quite charming; he thought immediately and took off his hat.

Inspector Sally "Inspector Sally Madame! I was just waiting here, I shouted many times but there was no one… "

Andria was now saying goodbye to her client, whom was apparently serving at the time the inspector entered the store and after closing the curtain behind her, walked towards him.

Andria "Do you have a lighter, Mr. Sally?" and put her pipe in her mouth waiting for him to light it.

 Inspector Sally "I apologize, I don't smoke!"

Andria "Don't apologize Mr. Sally" and took a lighter from the pocket of her dress and lit it. "So, what brings you to our neighborhood? Are you a fan of antiques? "

Inspector Sally "I am not, although some objects in here, aroused my interest, I confess. The lady who just left, was her your client? Is there another shop within this shop, madam »?"

Andria "Andria! My name is Andria. And yes there is a small room right behind us. I was reading the cards for the lady you saw. If you want I can read yours inspector!" she told him with a smile on her face.

Inspector Sally "I'll pass, thank you! In fact, Mrs. Andria, do you have permit for this extra room of yours? Or a license for medium services that you provide? "

Andria "I don't suppose you will arrest me inspector… just for trying to pay my rent. Antiques do not always make enough money, so I have resorted to other services."

Inspector Sally "No, that wasn't my intention. That is not the reason that brings me to your shop, Mrs. Andria. I am afraid that it is something much more serious."

The woman's look became serious betraying her emotions and she immediately turned it away and looked at the armchairs next to him. Then with a confidence in her voice she invited him to sit down.

Andria "Well, don't keep me in suspense! Please tell me the reason which brought you here tonight." she said as they sat in the armchairs and she deeply inhaled the smoke from her silver thin pipe.

Inspector Sally took a small vial out of his trench coat pocket that looked like a small perfume bottle like the ones in the window and placed it on the table in front of them.

Inspector Sally "This!"

Andria "I don't understand you."

Inspector Sally "I really hoped you'd understand, my dear. Everything would be much easier you see! "

Andria "Explain to me so that I can understand."

Inspector Sally "This little bottle contained concentrated liquid from Mandrake roots. Mandrake is a plant with healing properties but also extremely dangerous if used by the wrong hands. You see my lady the amount of liquid this tiny bottle contained can kill you and me, in seconds if consumed. Do you know the origin of this vial? "

Andria "How do I know inspector where this liquid was found? My own bottles contain perfumes only; I do not sell filters and magic herbs to the world."

Inspector Sally "Too bad I thought I was dealing with a smart woman. This Mandragora was the cause of the death of an innocent woman and the child she was carrying in her womb, Mrs. Andria. Now I do not know how much money your customers give you for such compounds but they are definitely not worth the years you will spend in prison. That is why I advise you to speak immediately so as I won't have to spend the day tomorrow again in your neighborhood with an arrest warrant and a much worse mood! "

Andria "You cannot relate this bottle to me, Mr. Sally. You have nothing! I'm afraid I'm going to let you down."

Inspector Sally "This is true! I can't relate it yet! But I have people who are ready to testify against you for other similar bottles that of course did not cause the same harm but surely the judge will take it into account when announcing your years of imprisonment. I may not have information about this bottle Mrs. Andria but do you honestly think that the court juries will believe you? Especially when the person to whom you sold it hangs on a thread not to lose his sanity and finally confess?! I wish I had your faith," he said and picked up the bottle again in his pocket. Then he got up and straightened his coat, put on his hat and headed for the exit when...

Andria "I did not know what he would do with it. I didn't know the girl was pregnant... I found out from the news. "

The Inspector stopped and the woman continued.

Andria "He came last November and asked about Mandragora. He had already done his research but wanted me to confirm that the procedure does not hurt at all for the one who drinks the potion. He will just sleep once and for all. It can cause convulsions and hallucinations I told him, but no pain. So when he was sure I gave him the bottles, he paid me and I never saw him again. I understood what happened when I saw the news. What will happen to me, Mr. Sally? "

The inspector's eyes, that were looking out on the street while the woman was talking, smiled and after he turned seriously to the antiquarian who was now being handcuffed.

Inspector Sally "Let us hope that the juries will feel sorry for you, Mrs. Andria. Or God! "

They left the small antique shop and headed for the car. He made the woman sit in the back seats and as soon as he sat in the driver's seat he went to start the car but suddenly stopped. Frightened, he turned to the woman behind him and asked her with his eyes wide open.

Inspector Sally "You said, you gave them to him!"

Andria "Yes."

Inspector Sally "Didn't he just buy one bottle?"

Andria "No. He specifically asked me for two. "

The Inspector quickly started the car and, obviously confused, started for the killer's house. He quickly developed speed and passed some red lights. Andria behind him did not understand what had happened but sat speechless and somewhat frightened by the sudden change in the inspector's behavior. Until she heard the radio and understood.

Inspector Sally "To all units. This is vehicle 583, heading to West 75th Street, and home of Sean Bailey. The suspect is dangerous to those around him and a threat to himself."

Police in the area responded to the inspector's call and headed for Sean's home. The inspector completed.

Inspector Sally "I do not want to be confirmed but I think he will try to commit suicide. He may have already done so, call an ambulance and report possible poisoning. Over! "

The inspector glanced at the detainee behind him who retaliated with her own cold, almost inhuman gaze. Thus showing no trace of repentance. Twenty-five minutes later, they arrived in front of Sean's residence and the ambulance and three other patrol cars were already at the scene. The inspector got out of the car and took the gun out of its holster. He ran to the entrance where he found two other police officers and entered the house. In the hallway he met a colleague who told him with a lowered gaze that they did not arrive on time. Now two paramedics were carrying the body of Sean who appeared to be sleeping. He stopped the stretcher in front of him and asked them.

Inspector Sally "Did you come on time?"

Paramedic "I want to believe yes but we can not be sure. It depends on how much he wants to fight. You may have saved his life when you prepared us for poisoning. We also found this vial on the floor. Mandrake. I guess you knew that! He is stable but we have to go."

The Inspector went to the living room and grabbed a small piece of paper that was on the table in front of him. He sat on the living room couch and put his hands on his face in a gesture of despair. He had not arrived fast enough. As bad as the news he told Jamie's mother later that afternoon were, were however liberating for her. Mrs. Lucy wept for her lost daughter and for the husband who took her life. She knew the killer and that gave her peace in her nights but it would not bring her child back. Love blinds she thought. Did her daughter live true love? If only she knew the answer to that. She was later informed of the piece paper Sean left behind.

'I went to find my Jay... You will never feel how much I loved her.'

Redemption

Two years later... New York

An elegant black-dressed lady with red hair and black branded glasses climbs the stairs and walks through the door of the psychiatric institution. The tight skirt she wears allows her to take small steps and the bag she has on her shoulder looks quite heavy in her attempt to change arms. The woman walks with confidence and her fit body does not testify to her age. She seems to be aware of the place around her and is heading to the psychiatric ward. There she arrives at the reception with the guard and wears a label indicating that she is a visitor. The guard smiles and opens the door.

Guard "Good morning Mrs. Brody, as every day, consistent in time for the today's visit! I wish my mother cared the same! Please come in!"

Mrs. Brody "Thank you George! Where do they have him today? " she asked him as they now passed through the common hall with the patients.

Guard "At the same place I'm afraid, Mrs. Brody. He did not even communicate with the nurses on lunch time. It's been a long time, maybe you should start accepting it." he told the woman accompanying him and opened the door of a room. Then he continued "If you need me I will be here. Just call me! " and closed the door behind him.

The room was relatively small with a bed stuck to the pistachio wall, a nightstand next to it and lots of photos of a couple hanging on the walls. There was also a locked window that you could not open and in front of her, in a chair, there he sat...

Mrs. Brody "Good morning Sean! How are you today?" said the woman in black and pulled up a chair to sit next to him. Then she stroked his hair and wiped the tears from his eyes. Sean sat motionless in front of the large window, looking up. The tears on his face meant that he understood the presence of the woman in his room but he still could not speak to her.

Inspector Sally, meanwhile, was walking through the door of the asylum and heading for the reception.

Guard "Good morning! How can I help you?"

Mr. Sally "Good morning! Inspector Sally, visiting Sean Bailey. "

Guard "Ah! What a pleasant surprise. You are the second person to visit him today. Mr. Bailey usually has no unexpected visitors. A few minutes ago I accompanied his mother, please follow me inspector! "

Mr. Sally "His mother? His mother does not want to have anything to do with Mr. Bailey. She returned back in

Poland a year ago now with his father. I don't know who you let in, but this cannot be his mother." he told him and with quick steps the guard led him to Sean's room.

From the window of his door was now visible the strange visitor who was now stirring the juice in which she had just poured a little white powder. Inspector Sally shouted the strange figure to stop and forcibly opened the door pulling out his gun. But as soon as the woman turned her face towards him, he stopped and put his gun back in its holster. Now he was looking at her in wonder and asked the guard to leave them alone.

Sally "Lucy? What are you doing here?"

Lucy "I was expecting we meet again Martin one day. How are you my dear friend?"

Sally "What did you throw in his juice Lucy? What are you even doing in here? " and took the juice from her hands.

Lucy "I come often and I see him. I pour lithium in his juice Martin, not to kill him anyway. Do not worry." and she took the juice from his hands again and drank some of it herself. Then she continued...

 "You see? No poison there! He has nightmares and he constantly paints of my Jamie. He has not forgotten her and he is so eagerly waiting for God to allow him to go and find her. He is suffering Martin. Lithium helps him... helps both of us... to forget! " she said and stroked Sean's hair, which sat motionless and speechless in its spot.

"He is suffering! And he will suffer for a long time to come.
" she said again and grabbed her bag and coat to leave.

Sally "But how is it possible? After the pain he caused
you? Do you still care about him? "

Lucy "Always! He was also my child Martin. And now I
have lost both."

The woman opened the door of the room and got ready
to leave but stopped when Sally whispered the following
few words.

 "*You will never feel how much I loved her!* Inspector Sally
remembered Sean's last words on the piece of paper he
had left behind that day. "Lucy, he wasn't right!"

She smiled at him and closed the door...!

Mandragora Autumnalis